Lost Liv
By
LISA JACKSON

ACKNOWLEDGEMENTS

I would like to thank everyone who helped and supported me.

DEDICATION
I would like to dedicate this book to my friends.

PROLOGUE

ATLANTIS 10,000 B.C.

She was walking away. My heart went with her. What I would not give to hold her again. Too have my home Atlantis safe and her people unharmed. But this is not to be.

PRINCE Ian

I can still remember the taste of her lips. Will I ever be able to forgive? Or forget?

I am Prince Ian, the pampered and indulged son of a king, the only son of a king, and heir to the throne. Indulged I say, incredulous. I have wanted one thing in my life! The thing he wanted me to want the most. Now I cannot have her. I am desolate, and he just sent her away.

I reminisce, remembering the sway of her hips, her well-rounded behind, and the feel of her lips molded to mine. The way we fit together so perfectly, as if the gods intended it that way. No, not so pampered or indulged. I feel outraged by my father's snide remark. *Yes, Father, I should be learning statesmanship instead of spending my days in carnal bliss with the woman I love.*

"Ian, my son, we must find you a suitable wife. You may have all the mistresses you desire, take them any way that pleases you, but until you obey me and marry, you will not have anyone to service you in your bed. Man or woman."

I was greatly offended that my father proposed I would want a man in my bed. He said this to demean and emasculate me in front of his vast council.

"Father, your majesty, your wisdom is known the world over. Surely you know I prefer only women?"

The king smiled, "Maybe a month or so alone would solidify your mind and remind you of your duties, without that lovely maiden to

LOST LIVES

Table of Contents
CHAPTER ONE
CHAPTER TWO
CHAPTER THREE
CHAPTER FOUR
CHAPTER FIVE
CHAPTER SIX
CHAPTER SEVEN
CHAPTER EIGHT
CHAPTER NINE
CHAPTER TEN
CHAPTER ELEVEN
CHAPTER TWELVE
CHAPTER THIRTEEN
CHAPTER FOURTEEN
CHAPTER FIFTEEN
CHAPTER SIXTEEN
CHAPTER SEVENTEEN
CHAPTER EIGHTEEN
CHAPTER NINETEEN
CHAPTER TWENTY
CHAPTER TWENTY ONE
CHAPTER TWENTY TWO
CHAPTER TWENTY THREE
THE END

warm your bed every night. I hear she is exquisite. Perhaps, I will send for her myself."

At those words, I felt a rage in me, building like an inferno. No one would touch her soft skin; place their lips where only mine had touched. She is mine; she has branded my soul with one night. I will never give her up; she gave herself to me.

LIRA

I thought he was different, but what everyone said was true. As soon as I gave myself to him, he sent me away like a common courtesan. He didn't even have the integrity to tell me himself, he sent a manservant to do the deed for him. Now I can never make a decent marriage.

I wish I could forget who I am or whence I came from. I am ruined. I will not let him know how hurt I am. I will walk away with my head held high. I look out over three concentric rings, with water in between, encircling our beautiful city, separating the nobility from the common people. And I am not nobility. I don't belong here. I never did. I let Ian talk me into living here. I was released by the king to find my own way. He asked nothing of me except honest company.

Ian asked that I never lie to him, the Crown Prince of Atlantis. Too many people told him what they thought he wanted to hear, not wishing to offend their crown prince. I never treated him differently, until that night.

I was an orphan, no one knows from where. They found me floating in a ship, alone, almost dead. All I can remember is my name. That's all I have. The good people who took me in, gave everything to me. The people of Atlantis were rich and kindly, honest and forthright. Except perhaps, Ian. He seemed so, after our night together. I couldn't stop thinking about him. Out of nowhere, a messenger came and told me to pack and leave. Well, I would not stay where I was not wanted.

I endeavored always to live up to the example of the people that helped me, until disease came. The people, the family that took me in, died. The soldiers sent me to the palace, as I seemed immune. I was in awe of this King Minos. He was godlike in his power and demeanor. Robust, with dark blonde hair with a bit of gray. He had startling blue eyes, the same as the prince. In comparison, his son, Ian seemed approachable and well, in all honesty, desirable!

I would have gladly sponged him down with cool water or held a goblet of wine to his perfectly sculpted lips. He was blonde, the same color as the beautiful throne he stood by. His piercing blue eyes glowed, and he was bare from the waist up. He looked impressive. It made me want to know what was under the sarong, made from cloth of gold.

I am a maiden, never having thoughts thusly. Now I know what happens when you wonder, don't I?

CHAPTER ONE

Prince Ian

A disease swept over Atlantis; we weakened from the sickness. I was the crown prince, it was my job to care for our people, but all I cared about was the beauty that stood in front of me. I had never felt such an attraction to anyone before. I wanted to keep her safe, lovingly tucked away in my bed, safe from the fates; safe from what was in store for us all.

She had long, lovely mahogany colored hair, violet eyes, and kissable lips. Her beautiful body just sSladeting to strain against the thin fabric of her white gown. My mouth was watering. I wanted to taste her through the material. I wanted to hear the angel speak. I knew her voice would be like the sound and song of the water around us; the melody we all lived by. I wanted to make her body sing to that melody. I could not take my eyes off her.

My father said, "Girl, what is your name?"

Lira, my lord. How may I serve you?"

"I am told this disease that ravages our Kingdom of Atlantis did not touch you."

"This is true, my Lord." she replied and cast her eyes downward. I hoped that I would not catch her eye, due to the very immodest thoughts in her head.

The king replied, "I will have you study with my healers and see what makes you immune."

"Of course, my Lord."

The king asked where he could send compensation for her services.

"My Lord, I have no one. I was orphaned on your shores, and the gracious family who took me in died of this horrible disease."

"Father, I have need of the services of a healer," I said. "She may stay in my royal apartments to make sure that all is well. I have lost two servants already."

All I really wanted was to get her alone, rip that dress off her with my teeth. My mind spinning at the thought of it. She was built for love...the swell of her hips, the curve of her legs, the sweet look on her face. I wanted to hear her scream my name. I wanted to hold her kissing her. I could not keep standing there with my my heart in my hand, in front of the entire court, imagining what delicacies she had to offer. I had to find a way to get close to her, but not seem as if I had an ulterior motive. I was the Prince of Atlantis. I didn't need a reason. I would simply request her services.

CHAPTER TWO

King Minos
I could almost feel the sparks between my son and that girl. At least I knew he was not gay; just particular. That would be a good quality in a future king, but so was producing heirs. Surely, he understood he could be with whom he wanted, but he should marry and have heirs for the Atlanteans. I would send word out to other kingdoms to find a suitable match for my son. Once the disease was contained, he would have no more excuses. There would be a royal marriage. There were plenty of lovely, women with big dowries and royal blood. A strategic alliance with our neighbors in Greece perhaps. The Greeks, our loyal cousins, were always putting girls forth.

There was a commotion in the outer terrace. What could it be? Didn't Atlantis have enough problems? The guards were talking in low voices.

"Platiius, go see what the guards are whispering about, and bring me news. I have other things to attend to on this day."

Platiius, the king's servant, ordered, "Let me through, I say. The king wants word of what transpires here."

A man was kneeling in front of the guard, his face bloodied and worn.

"What has happened?" Platiius asked, "what brings you to court in such a state?"

The man replied, "My Lord, there is land disappearing in the fishing villages."

Platiius snorted in derision. "Whatever can you mean land is disappearing? Perhaps you had too much wine? Were you facing to the ocean instead?"

"No, my Lord truly. Poseidon himself must have opened the gates of his realm. I myself felt the ocean quake and heave. We flailed about in our boat, and as we watched, the ocean swallowed a piece of land with many houses and a fishing dock! My Lord, I must speak with the king! His good people are dying a most horrible death. We must know what we can do to stop this!"

"I will take your request to the counsel," Platiius said. "First we must see proof of what you say."

"I am but a humble villager and fisherman, but I am an Atlantian." the man responded.

"When does our word not stand as surety?"

Platiius replied, "These are desperate times. Disease kills many every day. We are beset on all sides, with requests for help and succor from all our neighbors. We must err on the side of caution. I will send the guard with you, he will stand surety, and I will bring this before the king myself."

The guard and the fishermen left. Platiius wondered. *Who has angered the gods so? Perhaps it is time to collect some riches and head away. No, I will wait. Greater riches will fall into my hands as the disease spreads. If I can convince all that the king and the prince aren't fit to rule, cursed by the gods themselves, perhaps they might see a way in the king's loyal advisor.*

CHAPTER THREE

P rince Ian
Ian paused in the doorway. He backed into the shadows.
I must see what's going on. I need a diversion from the thoughts my lower extremities are having. This fisherman sounds desperate. Could parts of Atlantis be disappearing? Does it have anything to do with this sickness so virulently spreading? Are the gods punishing us? As the prince, these are my people. I am sworn to protect them. I must do something.

Ian heard Platiius talking to the guard and the fisherman.

Can this even be true? How can whole pieces of land disappear? Whole villages? Into the sea? There would be something left surely? Bodies, pottery, clothes, something? Could there be any other reason? Perhaps the man weaves a tale to get coin?

Ian pondered this for a few minutes.

I can think of no gain that would issue from such. What could make whole pieces of land disappear? Surely, no one has greatly offended the gods? We make tribute, we worship, and we hold the games. Perhaps this fellow's land was too close to the sea, wasn't shored up well enough. Still I can't imagine such a fantastic tale. Why would he not go straight to my father with this information? Surely, this man deserves audience.

He listened as Platiius ordered the guard to go with the man, and motioned to another guard,

"Find out where this village has vanished. If it has, bring back a report and anything that is of value. You and I will make equitable arrangements this evening. Did you find out if the nobles in the south palace have gone for the day? Make sure you stop in. If they are gone, plunder as you will. We will blame it on general unrest. Take care to be seen in uniform, then you can be safe saying you are on the king's business as I have ordered, from the mouth of the King Minos."

Ian stepped back into the shadows.

Platiius the plotter. As always his is scheming for himself. I have always suspected him a thief, but to stoop so low. I am outraged! He is stealing from the dead, hoarding their wealth, and planning to escape with it. He would betray his king? His people? What else does he know? I must go straight to my father with this woeful tale.

Ian turned to leave. A light touch brushed his arm. He spun around, and as he did, the aroma of honey and warmed brown sugar seeped into his senses. He looked into her violet eyes, appreciating all the scenery that she was.

"Your Highness," she said breathlessly. "The king has sent me to find you. I am to be your servant, I will be at your disposal, but right now you are needed in the throne room."

Ian looked her over appraisingly. *Oh, she could serve me in so many ways...on her back with her knees bent and tucked up, on her knees, while I fist her hair. I'll drive my tongue deeper down that honey-tongued throat, listening to her moans from that oh so sultry voice she just used on me, telling me she will be my servant. Could I get it out of my head? I think my will power will shatter if it touches anything but my body at this moment.*

His mind wandered further. *I would like to take her . Would she turn her head and look at me with those intense violet eyes as I pulled her too me? I want to watch her hair caressing her shoulders making a veil of her face. The gods have truly blessed me, or cursed me.*

Ian headed back to his father, then wheeled about.

"You will be in my quarters when I return. I wish red wine and sweet figs to be ready."

"Yes, my Lord," she said modestly, with her eyes downcast.

"I do not want to hear you went to the healer's' quarters first either. Do you understand? I do not wish to have the plague spread about. They told me you were immune to this disease, but that does not mean you will be immune to something else! That is why there is the healer's' quarters. I am not in any mood to be trifled with, do you understand? Atlantis is beset on all sides. I will need some rest."

And some much deserved respite from my aching lower half.. Of course, I do not say such things to her. She does not need to know what feelings she has roused in me. Curse their timing too. I can hardly walk around the palace with a tent in my sarong. If she noticed, she has given no sign whatsoever. She has not even looked up. Now my imagination burns to know why she is so cowed. Has someone hurt her? I would not harm her for all my brash words. I feel a rush of rage that someone might harm her in any way.

She then says, "Yes, my Lord is there anything else you desire?"

"There is, we will discuss it later."

Oh yes, I think to myself, we will discuss much. Well maybe not so much talking. I prefer her to be busy with her luscious mouth in more entertaining and pleasurable ways. Those full lips sliding slowly against my own, as her lovely violet eyes sSladee up at me. I stumble; then shake my head to clear it from this reverie. What is wrong with me? I have just met this girl. It's like she crawled inside my mind and keeps feeding me thoughts. I must leave her presence now. She is like a drug in my system. I have to have a clear head, both of them!

Ian headed back to his father, in the throne room.

"I cannot accept that!" King Minos yelled. "I will not believe the gods have abandoned us! We make sacrifices and we help our neighbors. We don't make war with anyone. Tell me Platiius, how have we erred? What do your oracles see?"

"I have it from my own healers that this plague sent to us was nothing more than a test." Platiius said. "A harsh test albeit a test just the same. The oracles my Lord, they say great riches must be delivered to appease the gods. They say we have become self-important and do not worship as we should. Some even say you yourself said there were no gods, no one greater than yourself, my King. The oracles said that was blasphemy, my Lord, and now the gods punish you. This disease and all the loss of life, the loss of our kingdom itself for man's greatest folly, his vanity. You must pay all you can, my King. You must save us all. Humble yourself to the gods. Give them your wealth and all you can round up. Bow low before the gods. Save your people if you can sire! I beg you! We all beg you!"

The court looked at Platiius as if he had sprouted another head, gasps were heard everywhere, some people fell to their knees.

The king said, in an extremely controlled, low voice, "I know not where your oracles get these stories! I have never once put myself above the gods! Never have I put myself before any god! I know not whence these stories come. I would do anything to save our people, our kingdom!" He strode quickly over to the open veranda. "See the god Poseidon himself bigger than any man with his trident of gold, pearls, rubies, and sapphires, his flashing eyes of fire opals! I will make any sacrifices required to save Atlantis and our people, but do not say I blaspheme the gods again! I will have your sniveling little head as a sacrifice! That I do swear to the gods and everyone here! Listen to my oath and remember this day! Your king would offer everything he owns to save you, and your homes! Rest assured, I will conduct serious inquiries into all these matters and see them righted, or die in the trying. That is my oath."

King Minos walked to his throne, and called for wine, seeming visibly to calm himself. Before addressing the court, his servants brought the wine. The people were murmuring. Looking around, he took stock of the situation. After giving his promise to protect his kingdom and make all right, Minos wondered how he would uphold his sworn oath. He then hit upon an idea.

"The girl, Lira, we took her in, gave her shelter in our home. Maybe she is sent from the gods. She has no illness, nor memory. I find that highly convenient. How is it we are to be in ruin in three days? A mighty kingdom that has stood for centuries. How is it to happen? If you don't have an answer, find one! If you cannot find one, then go from my sight and spout nonsense somewhere else. I agree to make more sacrifices from my own personal wealth. Any of you who wish to make sacrifices are encouraged to do so."

The king fell silent as he contemplated what else he could do.

CHAPTER FOUR

Prince Ian

"You summoned me, father?"

"Yes, I surely did, as the crown prince of Atlantis, you should know the dire straits prophesied for us."

"No, father, I have not heard. Is there a new sickness? What would you have of me? I am yours to command, as always, my King."

"No, my son, it is not something you can do for me. It is for our people. Our very way of life hangs in the balance. I am told the fates have decreed Atlantis will be gone in but three short days. The oracles say I am the cause of the gods' anger, but I swear to the mother of the gods, Queen Hera, I have not done so. I have sworn an oath to make this right. To help our people and our kingdom. If you were king, what would be your orders?"

"I would find the source of this knowledge," Ian said, looking sidelong at Platiius, "and make sure it is a reputable source. I would take much counsel. I would pray deeply and meditate with our priests. I would make more offerings to the gods. On the morrow, certainly I would send trusted men, to all the corners of our kingdom for an accounting of all circumstance. And of course, contact our neighbors and allies. You never know when need will arise, and the time may come to call a boon. I would also set up posts with some guards, and some healers for aid."

"Ian, my son, sometimes you astonish me. I thought you had no mind for politics, and no desire to learn kingship. Well thought out, my boy. I am proud to call you my son on this day! Have the steward bring us more wine, we will wait here and watch the sun set on glorious Atlantis. We will find the truth of these matters. I have summoned the healers for a meeting this eve, would you attend and learn the grave import for our kingdom? Of the rightness of the matter? Or does the idea of the sweet blossom I sent to your service this day entice your thoughts hither? I would not blame you. Enjoy it while it lasts. I have sent messengers out to sSladet negotiations for a wife for you and fine grandsons for me!"

"Father, I would prefer to stay and hear the news of what plagues our realm. I have no need of a wife yet. I would not bring a new wife to a country stricken with disease. What chance your precious grandsons would live through that? Childbirth is travail enough, is it not? My brother died thusly, did he not? With rumors spreading of ludicrous things attributed to you, my Lord, no, now is not the time for nuptials. Now is the time for making Atlantis whole and strong again. To right any wrongs or slights, whatever they be. Let us fix what is wrong in our realm. I will then attend the needs of an heir. We have no idea of where the disease comes from or whom it will strike down, and adding this new dire threat that Atlantis will be gone in three days," Ian scoffed, "I hardly think we have time for a wedding."

"That is some strident defense you put up for your country, so dear to you now, when but two days ago, you couldn't be bothered for anything but drinking and sailing," King Minos commented. "Is it the wife that is objectionable to you or the duty that it entails? We all have our responsibility, you will shoulder yours, I have faith. Your quick turnaround today proves you an honest man, a caring man. You needed a crisis to bring you to terms with it. As far the wife, you don't know that a lovely princess from a foreign land would get sick. We know not from where the sickness stems. Well, we will appease the gods. We will hear the truth of it tonight. Come, drink with your father."

Sounds of horns blew in the distance!

"It is our outer garrisons, my King, they sound the alarm!" one of the guards announced. "Do we go out to aid in force or dispatch messengers to see what this is about?"

"Is it out in the far reach garrison? How many times did it blow?" King Minos asked.

"Four, my Lord."

"Are you sure?"

"Yes, my Liege."

"Tend to it then. That is the alarm for city sentries!" Minos commanded.

He turned to his son. "Ian this is an excellent opportunity to show your leadership abilities. What do you suggest, son?"

Prince Ian looked around at the assembled court, well aware of that fact he would be judged from that moment on. *This could be his defining moment. He thought to himself. We have so many problems right now! What needs addressing first? Our people are dying. The fishing villages are disappearing. The oracle has prophesied our doom. According to the oracles, from my own father's lips, our doom is sealed. Never have I heard him say such a thing. I know my father is proud of our kingdom. Where do I even sSladet? I find it rather expedient that Platiius says that the gods demand riches? More than we send now? After what I heard but a few minutes ago, I need to figure out who I can trust. I must save Atlantis and all her people.*

And why now, when all I want is to go back to my rooms and explore the delicate flower that awaits me and my every command. Even as I think that, my mind wanders and I grip my sword hard. What's wrong with me? I am not an untried youth with his first look at luscious, lovely flesh.

He jerked himself back to the present as someone coughed discreetly.

"Father, I decide forthrightly, I would send a fleet messenger to hasten the news back to us with any problems. I would also assemble the council in case the prophecy has something to do with this alarm, not the sickness perhaps. Maybe we are focusing on the sickness too much?"

"I agree son, send the messengers. We will meet in the war room for council and strategy. Call all the elders, our generals, and the head healers. We will make a plan of action and decide best how to appease the gods. Have the kitchens send in a feast, this maybe a long night."

My father was listening to me! Not talking at me like a child! I felt I could not let him, or our people down. I would be the prince needed in this hour. I watched as all the important men in our kingdom filed past me, not one patronizing glance. *I would be worthy of this, not just as my birthright, but because I would earn this on my own merits. There had to be a common reason for all these great tragedies that were happening. With the greatest minds in the kingdom working on it, surely we would figure it out.*

I groaned like a petulant little boy. After all my grand thoughts and plans, she popped right back into my head. I imagined her asleep on my bed, her hair slightly mussed, her long legs tangled in the sheets, the slight rise and fall of her chest as she breathed. Maybe she was a trial from the gods as some, including my father, had wondered. She was beautiful enough to be a goddess herself. I was afraid if she were a test, I would fail. I could not stop myself from thinking of her. It was driving me mad. In came the healers at last. They all bowed before the king, every one of them looking frightened, and they were carrying something.

The head healer Simioz, said, "My Lord, we bring many grave tidings. We have had a great influx of sickness as you know, and we can find no cure, as of yet. Some people have a cough that hacks out ill humors, in the form of blood. We have treated them with heated wine and herbs to help the pain."

Looking directly at the king, Simioz continued, "As of this moment, my Lord, I can find no reason for this illness. It may have been sent by the gods." Simioz fidgeted under the king's regard. "There is more Sire, more people from the outer regions have come to us complaining of stomach distress and distended bowels. We have studied this new problem in depth. It seems there is another thing at work here. Sire, may I present Iolios, from Atroplios?"

King Minos nodded his head in assent.

Iolios stepped forward cautiously and bowed reverently. "My King, I bring grave news indeed." He shuddered perceptibly. "I was out fishing not two weeks ago. I felt the sea heave underneath me as if a monster or a god was shooting up from underneath. I hurried to the side to see what was happening, but all I could see were bubbles, Sire, and I could smell an awful odor. Not much later, there were dead fish. I had to row through to get to them. I have never seen the like. Straight away, home I went, to check on my family, and make report. As soon as I got to the city, Lord, they were packing their things and told me to tell the guards my story. And I did, Sire. They sounded the alarms, and as we were talking, a wave rushed in and drenched us with the foul smell and fish. The water burnt, my Lord. See my arms. They are burned from the sea! What shall we do?"

The healer stepped back up and guided the man away with a nod from the king, who said loudly, "We will procure a way through this disaster."

The king walked about the room, all eyes on him.

Simioz returned, "May I speak?"

The king gestured to the seats right inside the doors. They were lovely white marble with shades of blues and golds on the padded seats.

"Restful at any other time, but today, I must deliver you grave news still."

"What could be graver?" the king asked.

Simioz said, "Some men from other fishing villages have brought their wounded and the fish. They say even a whale is dead, my Lord. I smelled these fish. They smelled of sulphur of the nether realm. What could kill a whale, my Lord? It must be the gods. We have brought the water and fish in case they may be of use. These poor people are coming to me. I can do nothing but ease the pain of their passing. There will be no cure unless the gods send one. This is far beyond my realm of healing or skill."

"Have the oracles anything new to say?" King Minos stood up.

"No, just send more gold, prostrate yourself."

"All these I have done, my friend, as I'm sure you are doing for our people. There must be some other way to appease the gods. I await more reports and my counsellors. They have yet to show up. Surely, we can convince the gods we are good people, or at the least give us time to evacuate, if it is the gods. What if it is a warring country? Has anyone thought that? What an easy victory to just scare us away!"

Platiius looked away quickly. *Yes, that does make it easier. Hopefully, they will all be running very soon. I would not like to be here over long myself, but the lure of riches is too much. All these whipped dogs will be running as fast as the sails or legs will take them! Then I will own all of this. I can buy whatever I want from here.*

He laughed evilly. People turned to stare. He forgot for a moment he wasn't alone, a situation soon remedied. They would all be begging him soon.

CHAPTER FIVE

L ira
Surely, I had come to the most beautiful place on earth. I could not imagine finer tapestries, softer down-filled pillows, gold gilded and painted walls. Looking out the windows, I looked upon the most beautiful white and gold city, with shining blue water in three rings, circling out from this, the main palace of Atlantis. You wouldn't know people were dying; whole villages being swallowed into the sea. If you believed the stories. I saw people fishing, swimming, going about life as normal, but I had seen the suffering of the sick. The family who took me in, they died not a week before. They suffered greatly; I cared for everyone until the end. I cried my eyes out as I buried poor little Kiaha, no more than a year old. She was as dear to me as my own child.

My family, as I knew them, included my father, Griud, my mother, Pollymia, and my little brother, Icura. They are all gone now, with many others I have known in the years I can remember. All good, trustworthy, smart people. Why was I spared? What happened to me before? What happened to leave me alone in a small ship with no memory except my name? Now I am in the same situation again.

Why, I asked Hera? My Lady, Queen of the gods, what have I done to give offense? I would gladly lay down my life to help heal people. Even as I was praying, I knew I was lying to myself and to the gods. There was something in me that whispered, gliding over my skin, gently lifting my hair in a caress of love. I felt, in that moment, that I would do anything to feel that caress again. I would always strain to hear what the whisper said; it was always elusive. I trembled when I thought about that caress. Would I ever feel something that was real? Was this all in my mind, what mind I had?

I laughed, trying to shake those feelings. I wanted to be good, truly I did. I was to await the prince, spoiled, self-centered, and obnoxious, who somehow made me feel something. Maybe it was his chiseled jaw or his tight sculpted abs that begged to be licked, or the beautiful sunlight hair, or the amazing startling blue in his eyes that made me want to drag him down to me and have him kiss me delirious!

My mind wandered to the many often-enjoyed pleasures I had seen others indulge in. What would it be like to have him drag me onto all those fluffy, gold-tasseled pillows? Would he take me roughly with no consideration for my condition, as I was untouched all my life?

Some had seen me as cursed as. My eyes are a strange violet. I had been shunned and spat upon for that alone. It was extremely hard to have no past, no lineage, no dowries, and on top of that, everyone who came near me had left. That I could remember. Except the caress that flitted against my conscience. Gods that I could understand.

Maybe I was to be with the prince. He seemed so spoiled, but maybe he was to be the one. With those godlike looks, gods knew, I would not be completely averse to it. But still, there was the caress. Maybe I was being wicked in thought, and that was why the gods saw fit to send me to that boy who ordered me about like a slave, a dog, to do his bidding. What did I expect? I came here to help with the disease that had taken all from me. Once again, I was left alone wondering what my place was to be in this world.

Why did I never sicken? Everyone looked at me as if I knew a secret cure, a remedy, a spell even. I was no witch, or magician, nor a healer. I was simply, Lira. Why it is everyone had a family, a destiny, a purpose, except me? I felt as if I were on the precipice of learning or being taught. Mayhap, I would learn the mystery of the caress, of the light brush against my conscience every day, seeming to want a way in. I knew not how to allow it, or deny it, but as I had been ordered to stay and serve the prince, it didn't much matter did it?

What did he want me to do? I was not to help the healers, though I was immune. He had more servants and sycophants than he could ever want. What could I possibly do that someone had not already done?

My mind wandered back to his sharp voice. It made me quake with fear, but also a slight moisture between my thighs. No, I cannot say I was immune to the prince's many charms. His rock hard abdomen that tapered down to slim hips with a tiny dusting of gold hair. He looked like a god, not the pampered princeling I heard he was. I thought of his lips issuing orders. I wondered if the tones in his voice would soften if we were to be intimate. Would he slowly entice me with his mouth on my neck, his tongue making a trail downwards towards my bosom, with his hands slowly, longingly exploring ahead? Or would he roughly shove me down and slide that gigantic swell I saw in his sarong right into me, tearing my very essence. Could he ever compare to the caress over my skin that I felt so often?

I had waited many hours. I wondered if I could eat from the golden plate. Would he be upset? Surely a few figs and grapes would be no harm, and a small glass of the red wine. I stretched out on the veranda with the gauzy white curtains blowing gently. The sun was setting. I felt a light sprinkle on my wrist.

CHAPTER SIX

Prince Ian
I was incredulous. *How could we accomplish anything in this kingdom? These counselors were worse than women were. All what ifs and buts. How did my father stand this nattering? When would the messengers be back! Why was the alarm sounding? Why hadn't the healers reported as ordered?*

Beneath this, I wondered, was the lovely creature in my room as I had ordered? Did she run off like the rest seemed to be doing? I was inclined to be very harsh with her if she was not where I ordered her to be. If I missed my chance to taste those lips, to run my hands through that beautiful thick, silky hair, bringing her up tight to me, I would be angered. I could smell her still. Why did she remain in my mind? I needed to take her and rid myself of the obsession. I didn't have time for that. Thank the gods I was sitting. All I needed was everyone to see my rock impatience for no apparent reason.

CHAPTER SEVEN

King Minos

My gods, what was happening? Everyone seemed to think the only solution was to sacrifice to the gods, as if we had offended them, or run to our neighbors for aid. Certainly, they would understand no one would grant the damned sanctuary or the sick. Where were my healers? I had ordered them to report hours before. They would certainly know what to do. They had enough patients to explain what ravaged the people of Atlantis. Had the gods truly turned against us?

We always made generous sacrifices and tithes to all the gods, Poseidon, always chief among them as our patron. Water walled us in and insulated us. Our very lives depended on the water around us. It nourished us; brought us wealth, power, and trade. Our people were happy, good people, well cared for. Could we have angered the god himself? What could we do to appease an angry god? We still had no idea what angered him. Maybe some could help if they ever arrived.

We should have consulted the Oracle. Where were my soldiers, my counselors?

"My King, I have grave tidings indeed," said the head guard that rushed in. "My Lord, permission to speak?"

"Of course, please tell me you have information on the alarms sounding in the city? What is happening?"

The guard spoke. He went on for some time.

I was completely bewildered by what I was hearing. I tried to dissect some of what he had just spewed forth; the great cloud, he said, rose from the ground to the heavens. Surely the work of angry gods. I rose and walked to the southern side view of the palace. It was all true! The gods spit gray clouds with burning embers down upon us. Even the sea roiled with exaggerated pain and displeasure. How could I stop this? What could I do to save our people? I turned to the guard, was there a full-blown panic? Was it possible to order an evacuation to our neighbors or one of our sister cities until we could be sure we had appeased the gods. Inside I shook to my core. I had never seen the like. I was almost mesmerized by the sight. What amount of loss could we expect?

Platiius ran in. "Your majesty, people are deserting Atlantis. They are taking anything seaworthy and leaving. They have been looting and pillaging, and many more unspeakable acts. I myself have seen some of our nobles carrying gold and jewels and getting into a fisherman's boat. I ordered them to stop. They told me the world was ending and they would find safe harbor from the destruction."

Ian spoke, "Father, what would you have me do? What are your orders?"

Ian was befuddled by my look of peace. I turned to him and said, "Walk with me."

Ian could think of no response, so he simply followed. As we left the great hall, commotion erupted. What shall we do! Where should we go? Many more yells were heard, and I paid them no mind. I was lost in thought, and Ian was also. This was not anywhere he had ever been in the palace. There was a beautiful prismatic light in the center of the room rotating ever so slowly. A mechanical spinning world. I turned to Ian.

"This place has been here since the beginning of time and shall be long after we are gone. It is space, it is time, it is the future, and the past. I tell you this now, because I will stay with our city. You will move this heart of our city to a safer location."

Ian believed me insane at that moment, but I continued. "Every king that has ever been born has been ushered into this room. You, my son, have come early and we haven't had adequate time to prepare. Did you see the mountain explode? Do you know what the dead fish and boiling sea mean? The coughing sickness? Our ancestors told me as I gazed out in awe at the sight before me. It is the bowels of the earth evacuating itself, shedding if you will. It will consume Atlantis, but there is a part of us that will live on as we have always done. Do you see that light that turns so slowly? The beautiful colors and the patterns one the walls?"

"Yes, my Lord," Ian answered.

I knew he did not know what I meant. I smiled tenderly at him. I sensed he was afraid and uncertain about what was happening, but I also hoped that when the time came, my son would rise to the occasion and do the right thing.

Suddenly, a humming transfixed us. It was coming from the suspended metallic object with Atlantis in the middle. I walked up to it, watching Ian walk around it, look under it, and above it, seeing nothing holding it where it was. He looked puzzled.

He turned to me. "It's getting louder."

"Evacuations sSladet now." I said. "Sound the five horns. You will return here by Midnight. I will have everything ready."

"But Father, where shall the people go?"

"Their elders know the safe places, the ones who have knowledge. They will go where they are most needed. Peru, India, many places, my son. Some will stay here."

I transformed in front of Ian. He knew it was me, although I no longer appeared the same.

"I will do as you ask, father, and I will return at Midnight."

Ian turned and a door opened. He marveled but did not comment. Within moments, we heard all the activity... the screams, the calm voices, the assurances, and the crying. He looked upon the throne where before, he only sat on my knee. I looked out upon my people and in a voice that was not like mine, I said,

"Gather together your important things and make for your designated place."

Ian shook at this pronouncement. Everyone seemed to automatically stop panicking and moved in a purposeful direction, as if a switch had flipped. Suddenly, there were only a few people yelling, and wailing. People hurried by, bowing on their way out. The council and healers walked into the throne room. They also bowed. "My Lord, may we pay our tribute before we leave?"

Ian was flabbergasted. What did they mean?

"Approach," I said.

These were men and women I had known all my life, but as they came to the throne, they all looked different. What was going on? I wanted to yell, but I had no voice of my own. Everyone dropped a small stone or piece of metal in the marble case next to the throne. Ian didn't look after they had dropped their tribute. It was as if they were erased from his memory. I knew he felt trapped inside himself. Panic was setting in.

CHAPTER EIGHT

Prince Ian
 Father should have been supervising evacuations, helping our people, not sitting there accepting some weird tribute. Maybe I had hit my head and this was all a dream? Perhaps I was sick! Deep inside, I knew that was not true.

I had that lovely maiden to take care of. What had happened to her? When Father regained control of his body again, he would see to her safety as well.

The ground was rumbling like a hungry stomach, then like the purr of a kitten. We heard human sounds such as pots clanging, people yelling and rushing. Where were they going? They seemed to all have a purpose in what they did. Had we become someone else in another world?

Father turned and looked at one beautiful side of Atlantis. It was white and golden with azure blue waters. The only mar was the people scurrying about. Upon the throne, he looked out the big veranda window and gasped. The lovely mountainside was gone. In its place was a horrid black column spewing into the sky making it dark. Shots of fire ejected every so often as if they are under siege. The sun was fading, the water was boiling, and whatever it had its hold on them was finally loosening.

I breathed heavily and felt horror at the sight before me. I wanted to flee, get as far away as I could. Abruptly, I rose, and remembered Midnight and Lira.

CHAPTER NINE

Lira

Something touched me. It tickled my neck. I tried to fall asleep, but there was a gentle rocking underneath me. It was lulling. I felt the light caress across my arm.

"Awake," I heard, whispered. No one was there. "Who calls to me? Do not play games!"

Getting angry, I said, "I am in Prince Ian's chambers."

I looked around seeing nothing, trying to clear my head. Wow, did the floor just move? Were the dreams I was having real? I ran to the window...still sunny and beautiful, stillness though.

I felt another tickle on my wrist. I looked down. There was a grey powder. What could it be? I straightened up and wondered when the prince would return. I cleaned all my dishes. I heard people yelling and moving about. I was told to stay put. What if there was a fire?

I ran out of the room to see what was happening and asked a few people what was going on. Not one person would stand and talk. I saw people leaving the palace with what looked like their belongings. Were we under attack? As I turned the next corner, I felt a dangerous lurch in the floor. I looked out the portcullis. My jaw dropped, the sky was on fire with a long billowing cloud from the ocean to the heavens! What could it possibly mean?

I had to return to the prince's quarters. Surely, someone would come find the prince and thus me. I thought we would all die here. Once again, there was the caress. I turned into it, hoping for any kind of answer. "Please I beg, who are you?"

"Dear lovely one."

I was so startled that I jumped back.

"I am but a well-wisher in awe of your beauty since the day you were born. I have followed you ever since. I keep you safe."

I thought to myself, I have finally lost my mind. No one has ever been with me all my life.

I said aloud, "Who are you?"

I was answered with a chuckle, "A god in love with love."

"What? The world is ending and that's my answer?"

"Do not be forlorn, little blossom. Your prince returns for you even now. I will not forget about you. Do not forget about me when you feel his touch. I can make you feel so much more."

"I don't think any of this is funny." I said. "Do you think blowing up a city is funny? If you have been around all my life, who am I? Why did you let me feel alone all these years! What kind of mischief and trickery is that? Doesn't my life mean anything?"

"Oh, my dear, you couldn't know who you were. The time has not come yet. You need to be ready for the next part of your journey."

"What was the first part? Can I know what that was at least? Who are my parents? Where do I come from? Is Lira my name? How old am I?"

I felt a caress on both cheeks.

"No, do not leave me, please." I begged forlornly.

That was the strangest conversation that was had that day.

Prince Ian stood in the doorway, watching me argue with the wind about who I was and was not leaving?

"Dear, please come sit with me a moment," he managed to get out.

I wheeled around, looking wide eyed. He indicated the long pillow next to him. I was so taken aback by the conversation I just had, that wasn't any stranger.

The prince breathed me in it seemed. His eyes closed as he held my hands loosely, with the gauzy white curtains swaying, and the sky slowly turning to Midnight in deeper shades of blue in the background. It was so surreal.

He was warm and smelled like sunshine and man. I wanted to smell more of him, the muskiness of him, and the taste of his skin. It seemed as if I had been waiting my whole life for that moment. He opened his eyes. I was struck with the intensity. We looked at each other while the world shook and rumbled around us.

He said, "Your name is...?"

"Lira, as far as I know."

"Whoever you were yelling at didn't tell you?"

He heard that? I could have shrunk into myself. He probably thought me crazy.

"Have you ever had another name?" He gently asked me.

"No," I shyly responded.

"Do you like the name?"

"I have never given it any thought, Your Highness."

"Feel free to call me what pleases you."

I looked down once again. I was staring at his sarong, not completely erect.

"I would like to spend a long night finding out what you like and do not like," he said.

I blushed furiously. "Whatever pleases Your Highness."

He said, "Call me Ian, please. I want no formalities between us."

"Can I get you anything, Ian? Wine, sugared dates?"

"No, thank you. Would you consider laying here with me a moment, watching this lovely city?"

"Not at all, my Lord, but if you get close, ash falls on you as if from a fire."

"Oh, lovely blossom it will be so much worse I fear."

I reclined. I felt his heart beating against my back, mine seeming to beat in time with his. I could feel his manhood against my bottom but neither of us made any move to do anything about it.

We felt more rumbling beneath our feet, and he held me a little tighter. It felt amazing... the warmth, the strength. I finally turned, feeling guilty. "Shouldn't we be out helping your subjects my Lord, I mean, Ian."

"No, my dear. They know what to do. I am to bring what's important at Midnight. What's important to me is you."

He tipped my face up and captured my lips in a kiss that seared me and bound me to his soul.

"How can that be? You don't know me."

"Do you deny you are the other half of my soul?" he asked.

No, I felt complete. But, how? I did not know, nor did it matter. He ran his hand down my back. I had goosebumps at the feel of his flesh on mine. He pulled me closer, licking along the side of my neck. He nibbled at my ear, breathing deeply in and blowing a hot trial everywhere . Oh gods, I thought, nothing had ever felt so good. Then his hand lowered slowly down my shoulder.

WHICH HE LIGHTLY RUBBED across as he was nibbling his way down my collarbone. I thought I should move in some way, but I was frozen at what he was making me feel. He moved more of his upper body towards me. I arched my back as his lips made contact over the fabric. His chest rubbed deliciously against mine. I still wanted more. I was not sure what I wanted though, or how to ask for it.

"Ease back on the pillows my love."

His words made my blood heat and heat inside. I laid back with the world ending in my view. He eased off my dress, licking a path from one to the next, I ached as he went from one, to the other. He grabbed the pitcher of wine. His sarong was nicely tented. I smiled in satisfaction. The air was getting thick.

"Let us moisten things up," he smiled mischievously, pouring wine on my chest, licking it off. He poured some in my mouth where his tongue was fighting mine for possession. He ran his other hand down my thigh. It was quivering, and I couldn't stop it.

"Lovely Lira, you're making me ache. I can hardly stand the pain. I have been thus all day. Do you see the effect of just your smell on me? The taste has made me crazy."

He took my hand and placed it on his chest. It was big, frighteningly so, but it was also warm and soft, and silky.

"This is for you, if you're willing. I do not force anyone," he said.

He was still toying with me and ripples of excitement were running through me.

"Ian," I said, "no force will be needed here."

He smiled, one of the most beautiful things I had ever seen. He ran his hand down my stomach, making it quiver and suck in.

He laughed. "Touchy little thing, aren't you?"

I smiled and said, "I do not know, my Lord. Am I?"

He looked down at me intently. "You have never known a man?"

"No," I replied, blushing furiously.

"How can that be? You're more beautiful than any other. You put Midnight to shame with all her blacks, blues and twinkling shades."

I smiled. "What a flatterer. I remember you said something earlier, about Midnight?"

"No need to worry about that now," he said. "First, I will show you what is happening outside."

I looked at him, very confused. His hand again tickled my ribs then circled my belly button, then over the curve of my hip. I was all feeling. Every nerve was alive.

The world seemed to narrow down to one feeling. I was so focused, I felt like inside me was about to burst. Ah. He took his hand away. I almost cried at the loss. He moved down my body.

"Do not worry my love. You will have what you're seeking."

He then proceeded to be everywhere but where I needed him. I reached out, seeking something. I found and fisted his hair. My hips were lifting on their own. I had almost no control. He finally dipped his tongue in for one long, leisurely stroke.

Oh yes, yes, the sensation was very intense. He lovingly licked each lip, inside and out.. Ah, I could not stand anymore! He was making slurping noises. Once again, my body tightened up. I didn't know what the feeling was, but I was so ready to feel, He licked my bottom lip biting a bit.

He said, "Easy love."

He pulled away again.

"You taste like honey and melted brown sugar. I could taste you all night, but we do not have that long. We have till Midnight."

I begged, "Please!

"Please what, little one?"

"I am not sure," I said.

The world was going up in flames and tremors all around us. It felt as if my body was trying to go with it. He smiled tenderly; I was doing it right! He put the his lips on my lips. I was unsure, so I slipped my tongue out and lightly licked him.

He said, "Do you want to be done here?"

I shook my head no.

He said, "Good, little blossom. Give us a kiss goodbye."

For a moment, I thought he was leaving me. I tried to suck him back in. He leaned backwards for a moment. My hips bucked and nearly threw him off. I thought I might choke, but he slid out with a loud pop. Was I sucking him that hard? He took his time rubbing his hand on me everywhere on his way down. When he was back to the core of me, it was almost full night outside, though I knew it to be a few hours earlier. He licked me again, lifting my butt with his hands so he could get to every inch of me.

"I do not want to hurt you," Ian said, "so let's get you well prepared."

I could have screamed my frustration. Just as I felt that, I felt the caress. I tried to go still, but it was caressing my shoulders Ian licked and massaged me. Air was playing around my ears, down my arms, and back over my chest a bit. I heard a chuckle in my ear. "I'm always here."

I tried to catch the face; it was so close. I felt Ian so close, Oh yes, that was amazing, but still not enough. Ian suddenly sat up. The whole place rumbled.

He smiled, looked behind him at the cloud and fire.

"Lira, do you want to feel that?"

I look at him, confused.

"Ian, I already feel that!"

"No, little blossom inside you?"

I was speechless. I had no idea what he meant.

"Are you ready for what has been eluding you all this night?"

"Oh yes, please, my Lord!"

"Back to my Lord again? You must be in great need!"

He kissed me again. He slid his hand between us. I tensed.

"Are you scared? He asked.

"A little." I stammered.

"Do you see what happens around us? That will be how you will feel inside as I pleasure you and join you in my pleasure. It will be like the jets into the sky, but it will be my seed shooting into you, and your pleasure milking it out of me."

I smiled. It was a perfect picture.

"Are you ready?"

"Oh yes," I said.

He rubbed his throbbing cock through my wetness and up around my hood till my clit popped out. Then he jacked off slowly on it a bit. I was just nerve endings. All I could do was feel. He was moving towards my virgin core. He started to push in slowly. I felt pain. I tensed again. I felt the caress oh my god. I bucked upwards. He had broken the barrier.

He looked at me once. I nodded. He began to move slowly. The caress was playing with me again. I was going crazy. Ian played with my neck . I couldn't keep doing it. The sensations were too much. I felt someone behind me, sliding under my back. No one was there. I was leaning up. I could see Ian and me. I felt a thrusting against my back.

Hot air blew across both my body. I was staring up in the sky as a big explosion . There was a new hot sensation I could tell Ian felt it too. He looked at me wide-eyed. I started pushing up into him, riding them both. I didn't think anymore. I was just pushing and screaming my way towards the column in the sky. I heard wet bodies slapping together. I felt cool air go over myself, Then Ian rubbed against that spot and..

Oh, yes, that was it. Oh, my gods. I had turned into the column.

Ian was right, a big tight column with little jets of amazing pleasure pulsing everywhere. I thought I heard a moan behind me. Then Ian stiffened and pulled me up to his mouth, so when , he was in my mouth and filling me below. We lay panting. We caught our breath, as the mountain seemed to share our pleasure, erupting a prodigious amount itself.

Ian and I watched mesmerized for a moment. He kissed me hungrily. "Midnight comes soon. We must be on our way. Can you walk?"

I laughed, "Um, no."

He smiled. "It's alright, little blossom. I will carry you."

"To where?" I said.

"To another world. We will rule as King and Queen."

I felt the caress slip my dress up a bit. I wondered, would it always be this good? Would the caress always be there? Would I ever find out who I am?

I would find out at Midnight.

CHAPTER TEN

Lira

I had lost all grip on reality. I was indulging myself with a prince, and a well, whatever he was, because he was definitely male. I felt the ground quake again.

My prince said, "Time to go little blossom." He swung me up into his big strong arms as if I weighed nothing. I was blushing furiously.

"My Lord, you cannot be seen carrying one such as I."

He replied, "What did I tell you about calling me my Lord?"

He glanced down at me with arched brows.

"To call you Ian," I said, with a breathy sigh.

He smiled tenderly as we moved through the castle. A loud, thunderous boom went off in the distance. The outer wall fell into the palace pool right below it. It cracked the glistening blue mosaic tiles in the shape of Poseidon's trident. I could not believe what was befouling us. This was it. The end of Atlantis. I saw so many people running. I looked a little closer. They did not look panicked. They moved about with purpose. This was strange behavior indeed!

I turned my face to ask the...Ian, and I gasped. He did not resemble my Lord except for the eyes, still the same beautiful glowing blue, pulsing with power. I shuddered for a moment.

He looked down, "What is it little blossom?"

I was unsure what to say. I stumbled over a beginning. "Ian, I wonder do you, well, are you aware that you're changing?"

He looked down at me again. There was another horrific sound as if a teakettle the size for the gods had whistled, it is done. We all stopped and looked heavenward for a moment, and in that moment, I spied that snake, Platiius, skulking across the room. He was burdened with treasure and wearing more than he carried. He looked at my Lord, sneered, and said,

"Looks like we both got what we deserved."

My Lord Ian, said, "I guess that is so Platiius. I have a most beautiful, loyal, loving woman. You have...stolen jewelry. You are rich indeed. I hope it brings you some measure of happiness."

Plattiius replied, "Indeed, it shall buy me another life far from this place that has been cursed. I have served so long with no thanks, treated as a cur under foot. Now, I can buy my own kingdom! I shall give the orders and see men scurry to do my bidding. Spoiled, indulged child, you still do not see what happens here. Look out then on your world, it is ending as predicted. All you think about is your conquest. There are mightier forces at work here than your father."

His visage took on a look of twisted hatred. "I am well rid of that man. The king thinks too well of himself. All of my life, he has ordered me about; taken anything I cared for, with no thought, no care for my happiness! I will relish his precious Atlantis destroyed, as I have prayed for so long. The gods have finally answered. Where is he now, the great ruler, when his people need him so desperately! Gone to save himself. That's where! Now out of my way, boy!"

The prince looked at him and thought how very sad that this was all that mattered to him. I stood aside and let out a small sound as he shoved us in his haste. "What a horrible man."

I agreed and moved on.

CHAPTER ELEVEN

Prince Ian
She looked at me. I saw a light in her eyes. "Where do we go to my love?"

"You said so many things in your room; I confess I was not always paying close attention."

She blushed. I smiled. "Well, I guess you can be forgiven."

She sputtered. I laughed, "Calm down, little blossom. I was only making sport. I do not regret one second of it."

I inhaled the smell of her, honey and warmed brown sugar, those smells so enticing; I would never tire of them, or the delicate lilac smell underneath it all.

"How are you so different now?" She asked quietly.

I waited, trying to formulate an answer within myself. Indeed, I felt different, at peace somehow. Why? How could that be? My world, my country, my people were dying, or evacuated. Everything I loved was destroyed, except what I carried in my arms. I pondered this question.

"I feel different, older, more in control. Perhaps, I even look different like my father and his counselors. I do not know the answers, little blossom, but father told me to bring what is important to me at Midnight. Therefore, my Lady, I am. I can think of nothing more important to me than you."

CHAPTER TWELVE

Lira

L I looked at him curiously. He certainly seemed different from the arrogant boy of yesterday. I was so confused but this felt right, like I had finally come home, but where was everyone? Surely, we should have been helping people leave or find safety. The few people I saw are moving with purpose, not panic. Rumblings in the ground sounded more ominous, and the quaking was almost constant. I saw water rushing over the breakers.

"Please put me down my Lord, Ian. We must run." I pointed out the waters rushing inland. He turned slowly and looked but didn't set me down. If anything, he tightened his hold. Maybe it was sinking in and he would come out of this fugue state and feel something.

He sighed audibly, "We must get to my father. He said all would be well as long as I arrived by Midnight."

He pushed through the heavy palms displaced in the throes of the violent eruption. He turned quickly down a long corridor. I looked up. It was way past twilight; I did not think it was that close to Midnight. Who could tell with the sky on fire? My mind was wandering, as my Lord's seemed to be doing.

I felt a caress, did I not? There it was again, just under my hair, running along the nape of my neck. I was so distraught.

"Please put me down? I am only hindering your progress! Whether do you seek?"

Ian looked down at me, a smile lighting his face, "Have you found your legs?"

Guilty, I looked down. I knew it could only last a little longer. "Yes, and for some time. I feel safer in your arms."

"Why is that?" he asked me.

I wanted to shake him. "Look outside! We will die soon! All your talk earlier was lovely, and I will treasure it the few moments we have left. I understand it was just bed talk, don't you?"

He shook his head slowly. "Love, do not upset yourself. I spoke truly."

I wanted to smash something on his head. Unluckily, the hanging pot did it for me. Right as I was wishing it, lo and behold, the pot came loose from its moorings and cracked upon his head.

I rushed to my beloved, "Are you ok? Please be ok?"

Berating myself inwardly, how could I have thought such a thing? He shook his head and golden pottery shards and dirt fell to the floor. Dazed, he looked around.

"What has happened here?" he asked.

I sat next to him, holding his head, checking for wounds. Again, I felt the caress and an unbelievable chuckle!

"Did you do that?" I yelled into the air. "I did not truly wish him harm! I only sought to make him see the fantasy his mind has made for him cannot be. I am no queen and he is soon to be a prince of nothing!"

I was shaking with rage and fright. Ian stirred against me.

"I have lost my way." He looked a little frightened.

Was the boy coming back?

"Sire, what way? To what? Allow me to help you and quickly."

"Why do you keep calling me Sire? I have asked you not to."

I shook my head, stubborn, exasperating boy.

"Ian, what are we trying to find?"

"The room where my father is. I have never been there before today."

I must admit, I felt some confusion. He stood readily enough, brushing dirt from his golden hair, even with impending doom, I felt myself becoming aroused looking at him, stroking his hands down his belly. He was sweating. If it had not been so dirty, I would have licked the sweat from his body with great relish.

He spoke. "We must find this room with great haste, follow quickly, my love."

He turned the corner and went down a staircase deeper into the palace. My heart was beating like a hummingbird. When water rushed in, we would drown if we went downwards. I tried to say something, but he was so intent. The staircase ended. There was a smaller hallway, and by the smell of it, the kitchen was close. Surely, his father, the king, had plans to escape. He would provide for his only heir at least. He said his father commanded him to meet him at midnight with what was most important to him. He had said that was I. I felt a lovely warmth in my stomach. He wanted me. I thought it wonderingly. After all that time, someone wanted me, not just to clean up, but for myself.

A tickle ran up my arm. I shooed it away from me. The thought captured me as I hurried behind Ian. I felt a deep groan. How do you feel a groan I thought to myself, but that was exactly what happened under my feet. I empathized, the world must be in terrible pain from the birth that was going on outside.

Ian stopped ahead. A humming sound and a strange blue ethereal light came from the doorway up ahead. He slowed down, listening. He turned and smiled that heart melting, liquid making smile.

"This is it! Do you hear that?"

"Yes," I replied, "I hear it all."

He said, "The hum, like a dragonfly above the water on a summer's day?"

I smiled at his description. "Yes, I do."

Immediately he went to the door. Opening it he said, "Father? Father? My Lord?"

Nothing but the hum answered him! He walked around the room, slowly circling the small model of Atlantis and the blue light from a globe above us, only it wasn't blue, it was prismatic. Blue lights shot out every few rotations. What in the name of the gods was this? How was Atlantis suspended? There were no strings or wires. Just a big golden set of wheels that rotated around it. I was dizzy just looking at everything. I felt a deeper rumble than before. It felt as if a great giant was tensing up. Were we to be hurled off the planet? I had no idea what to expect next. Everything had gone insane in the past two days and maybe myself with it. I looked over quickly at Ian. He was still looking around forlornly for his father.

"Maybe," I said to him, "we should seek shelter away from here."

He briskly shook his head, "No, this is where we are to be. Surely, I did not miss Midnight."

I had nothing to say to that. How could we be sure what time it was? The sky was gone when we came down. Everything had been so surreal. I began to hope it was all a dream from which I would awaken, even the beautiful prince, who had branded my soul in one night. He was amazingly handsome, sculpted from the best clay, I was sure of that, every part lovingly carved to perfection. How I longed to taste and experience them all. I heard what sounded like a small child laughing quietly. I turned to find no one there. Was it the caress again playing a new game with me? So many questions, so few answers.

Again, I heard the giggling. I whispered to Ian, "Did you hear that?"

"What?" he said.

"That giggling. It is that of a small child."

He looked at me curiously. "No, I heard nothing. From whence did it come? Which direction?"

I shrugged helplessly. "I have no idea. I keep hearing it though. My Lord, Ian?"

He turned to me, "Yes."

Once again, it was as if I was staring at a stranger. Beneath his skin, I saw something. I could not find the words to describe it, but he was indefinably more.

"Do you remember why we came down here?" I asked him.

He said, "Of course, we leave Atlantis at Midnight."

I asked nervously, "Do you think we will live to see it? The earthquakes beneath us, the floor is heaving in places, I can no longer stand still and remain upright. Yet, you seem unbothered by the impending doom upon us."

"Ah, little blossom, do not worry so." He smiled. "I would let naught harm you. Coming into this room, I have somehow felt a completion in myself. I know not how it has happened or why, but there are things in my mind I know I never learned, a great wealth of information, such as I was never taught. See the spinning light above us?"

I nodded eagerly.

"I know its power source now," he said.

I craned my neck to look up. I could not even see where it ended or how it was attached. How could he have known? He was but a boy was he not, or was he? Once again, I was nervous.

The information was on the Akshua.

My Lord read from the page:

"Real power exists beyond the range of humans, since it is available to sensitive individuals' minds in altered consciousness within all living things. For energy, plants were not only for food, but also for the force in them that transferred into power. The Indians devised a means of transforming. Early in their civilization, when the bodies and minds fully aligned and balanced, the Indians perfected sonic levitation to lift large objects for use in the buildings and monuments. Employing intense group concentration to direct the energy from soundwaves, they raised and lowered massive blocks of stone without machinery. To accomplish this amazing feat, people linked arms and danced in circles to drums and cymbals around an immense boulder, chanting loudly in the prescribed manner. As they focused on the large rock, their intense mental strength combined with the pulsation of sound. Electromagnetic transducers are electric quartz crystals with special tones or other samples of energy. They are all strong ultrasonic vibrations above people's hearing. Sonar may help map ocean bottoms. It is a well-known use of ultrasonic waves. Imported properly, ultrasound is capable of increasing molecular motion and liquids, generating the cracking solids. It kills germs. Ultrasound is also a well-known diagnostic technique and provides images of internal organs. If the vibrations of ultrasonic waves were strong enough, they would kill animals and people, as equally powerful sonic rate is below people's hearing."

"If you know the power source, can you help Atlantis?"

He smiled. "Nothing can save Atlantis from what is happening right now. Let me explain."

"How does this paper explain anything Ian? I am more confused than ever. Where did this book come from? I saw no book in this room when we arrived. When did the table get here?"

Bewildered, I looked at the book again. I gasped, "Extraterrestrials?"

"The ice age. Yes, everyone knows that."

"What? The destruction of Atlantis? These dates tell of more things that have not happened yet. How is this possible? Is this the oracle's prophecy? Is it a reading?"

Ian seemed unaffected by this amazing news. He just flipped to the next page. I could hear a loud roaring noise, and I trembled inside myself. How could he be so calm? We would die soon, drowned or burned up, and Ian was talking crazy. What was worse, I could still remember the feel of his hands on me, his tongue licking down my stomach, and it caused another deep ache inside. I was truly insane to think of his chiseled abs, the feel of him inside me, and his fingers on me at the same time. I hoped he had not noticed my state.

Surely, someone would come to find the prince. Surely, they would need their prince or king. I knew not what else to do. I thought we should get out of that strange, otherworldly room. It seemed to be affecting him in an inexplicable way. He was the same handsome, princely boy, but it was as if an image had superimposed over another. Perhaps, I had hit my head as well. I longed to understand what was going on, almost as much as I longed to feel his hands upon me.

Thunk. Whirl. Hiss.

Ian spun around, as a door that was not there before, opened. Like the cowardly girl that I was, I ran and hid behind the prince. A man stepped out, an impossibly tall man with silver hair and...I gasped, glowing blue eyes.

CHAPTER THIRTEEN

Lira

Ian said, "Father?"

I peeked out again. Dear gods, it was King Minos. I was so befuddled. That was not who I saw step through the magically appearing door. Keeping my mouth shut, I dropped to the floor in a curtsey. "My King," I murmured.

Ian, not seeming to notice anything wrong with any of that said, "Father, I was worried. Where have you been?"

"Preparing our new homes," King Minos answered.

Ian shook his head briskly. "Excuse me, my Lord, but our home was destroyed."

Finally, I thought, someone had come to his senses.

King Minos said, "Did you read the book my son?"

"Only a few pages opened for me. Even now, I am unable to recall what the import was."

I was dumbfounded. Where was the man, who but minutes ago, explained all would be well and extraterrestrials would be coming to save us. I was unsure on that part as well.

The king sighed, "You must not be ready for the knowledge it retains. It will return when the time is right."

I glanced around from my station on the floor. Sure enough, the book was gone to only the gods knew where. I was so scared now. I felt the warmth of the caress over my shoulders like a hug. I smiled to myself, if I was crazy, it was in the best way.

Ian said, "Father, what shall we do? How will we save Atlantis and our people?"

The king gently took his son by the arm, leading him to the globe that was suspended. I knew not how the replica worked.

"This is our home correct?"

"Yes," the prince nodded.

"Water will soon overpower the inner buildings. It has already breached the outer circle and the army."

"Yes, Father. I have seen with my own eyes. It is close to us at the palace now. With every grumble from Mother Earth, Poseidon hurls water forth. I think to stop the burning earth and sky, but now, Zeus hurls lightning bolts from overhead. They are on fire and blasting out more fire bolts, smaller ones. It is as if the gods are having a war, and we are stuck in the heart of it. Perhaps they make war because of us. Zeus is maybe jealous over the attention lavished upon Poseidon and Mother Earth. Mayhap all of our dealings depending so heavily on water angered her. I do not presume to know the will or thoughts of the gods, but it seems to be the very case of which our counselors ascribed to you of doing."

I was listening intently, hoping to hear an explanation. The king opened the book to another page.

"I would have you understand this is not the work of the gods entirely. Mother Earth must sometimes give birth as all mothers do to keep the planet alive, and for that, some destruction needs to happen. Some women die in childbirth, like your mother. You are here to carry on her genetic line and mine of course, but there's more than that. We come from a long line of travelers. We have genes of the gods in us."

Ian gasped, "Father, you blaspheme."

"No, son, I tell truth. Look at me and tell me what you see."

Ian walked around his father, squinting, then happened to notice me, still on the floor. I quickly dropped my head.

He said, "I see you father, as I always have. Is this some test? I have brought what is important to me at Midnight as requested."

Ian turned to me and gestured in a sweeping manner. "This is all that is important to me."

King Minos chuckled, "Truly? No wine, no clothes, no weapons, shields, or books? That is not what I expected from you. Not at all. I guess you have made a choice. We shall see if it is a good one."

Ian spoke, "Please get up, Yew"ll, and meet my Father. Father, this is Lira". He raised me to my feet.

My cheeks burned in shame. I knew I must look terrible. I was being presented to the king for the second time with nothing to offer, as if I were an equal.

"My Lord King." I dropped a quick curtsey again.

He looked me over. "You are very beautiful, Lira. I hope you will find happiness. I have learned since meeting you, that you will be most important to us in the days to come."

I was dazed. The king had asked about me, and what did he mean by days to come? The world was ending.

"My Lord, whatever you require," I replied.

I glanced up quickly at Ian. He looked as confused as I was, but said nothing.

The king said, "We must be back to the arranging of things, and you are not as unlocked in mind as I would have you before the becoming."

Ian and I said in unison, "The becoming?"

"Yes," the king uttered, aggravated, more like the king we knew instead of the stranger of kindness with glowing blue eyes and silver hair from before.

WAIT! Neither of them had glowing eyes. They both looked and sounded normal, like Apollo, but human. Although Ian would always look mouthwatering to me.

I clenched inside thinking about the hours we had spent in bliss. How we promised things that could never be, but seemed real at the time. I thought nothing could ever take me from this man's side, except death, even though I would find him and follow him through any travail he might endure. A love as great as ours must surely be blessed by the gods. Why could I not keep my mind on the matters at hand? I was not a love sick...I felt the caress again. I was in love with a prince, and me, a nobody. This could never work out. He said I would be his Queen, and we would rule together in a happy place. His father would never allow a commoner to marry his precious son. Even I knew this much of this king.

Ian's mother had died giving birth to him. They say the king was so heartbroken, he vowed to the gods never to marry another, and for eighteen years, he had steadfastly remained true to that vow. It did not mean he had been celibate. There were no rumors of royal basSladeds, however. Maybe a love can be that true. I could only hope. Ian owned my heart as well as my virginity. I could only give him children and devotion for the rest of my life, what little there was left of it. Why was I the only one panicking?

"Ian," the king said, "There is much I have kept from you. One, because of necessities, and two, because there was no need for you to know. Now I must explain things to you, and we have no time. I wish things were different but they are not. I have to get you to accept the truth of things and very fast. Can you keep an open mind, my son, and listen before you question? There is much and no time. I may not be there for answers at the end."

Ian looked confused and began to speak, but as he did, there was a loud cracking sound as if three hundred cannons were going off simultaneously. It felt as if the entire palace was rocking. I stumbled forward into Ian's arms. He held me tightly. It felt as if the very floor had come alive like snakes squirming beneath us. Of course, my appetite had not dropped a whit. I was excited to be in his arms again. I would die happy. I thought. Surely, it was fright, not excitement. I could not lie to myself. I would let him take me now if he desired to do so.

I heard the small version of Atlantis clicking. I peeked over. It looked as if it was starting to glow, a blue prismatic glow like earlier. In the wall of the room was a map. Dear Gods, it was Atlantis and so much more. I did not think I was meant to see it, so I looked down. The king studied it, at those parts that seemed to be new, as did the prince.

"What does it mean? Father, I am very confused with what is going on right now. Can you explain the source of the power of the blue?"

"I can and so much more, but you're not ready to hear this. I must begin at the beginning, though we do not have much time. We come from a place so far away from here that time has no meaning. Getting here from our world took more lifetimes then we could ever imagine!"

Ian shook his head, "How could that be?"

His father explained. "We were put into an artificial sleep. We traveled long by a ship that flew through space, much as your ship glides through water. Our basic functions slowed, so we did not age. Of course, a few stayed awake during this period to monitor the life enhancers and to pilot the ship if needed. They gave their lives to get us here, to keep our culture alive as I am going to do now, and you, my son Ian, will travel far and make another new home for us. This home is lost."

Sadly, King Minos shook his head. "Our lovely home will be devoured and lost for so long that the minds of men will forget. They will search over land, under sea, and everywhere in between, but they will forget about between Midnight. And that, my son, is where our people and the new Atlantis shall be."

"Father?" Ian said plaintively, "You sound mad? Where has this crazy tale come from? I mean no disrespect," Ian says, "but surely, you must know how this sounds?"

I looked up at the two men, mesmerized by sight and words. What could possibly be happening here? Neither the king nor the prince looked the same. The more the king talked, the more translucent he looked. Perhaps it was a trick of the unearthly light, or mayhap, I was already dead and it was the afterlife. Maybe I was still upstairs, knocked out by the falling palace. Any of these options would have made much more sense to my terrified mind at that moment. I desperately wanted to speak up and call attention to the changes, for love of the Gods.

King Minos, said, "Come now, Ian, surely you have felt you have more potential locked inside you?"

Ian looked at his father. "Truthfully father, no, not until this day. With all the atrocities and indignities that the gods are sending to us, I truly did not feel even up to the task of being a prince. Ever since I laid eyes on this lovely woman, I have wanted to be better from the inside out. If anything truly made me feel like I was more, it is her doing."

King Minos looked down, "Come here child."

He held out his hand to help me up. I was afraid, but I knew that it might change my life. I took the king's hand and stood up as gracefully as I could with the floor quaking beneath me. It almost felt like the sway of a boat.

King Minos held my hand tightly. "Let me look at you, my dear."

He tilted my head to catch the light that enhanced my violet colored eyes, the golden hue of my skin, and the long tresses of mahogany colored hair with tiny hints of gold and copper.

He turned, still holding my hand, "Ian," he intoned.

Ian jerked as if shocked by his father's voice. "Yes, my Lord," he asked, sweating profusely all of a sudden.

King Minos looked at his son, not quite a man, not ready, but there was no time. As punctuation to that thought, there was a loud blast with an eerie sizzling sound with more small blasts at regular intervals. Everyone looked at each other for a solemn moment, standing still, listening to the earth tear apart around them.

"Ian," The king said again, very gently. "Is this woman the one that was brought before us yesterday? The very same who is immune to the plague, who was lost at sea, arrived here on her own, with no family and no memories? Do you remember anything, my dear?"

I shook my head. I remembered one thing with vivid clarity, I certainly was not about to mention it to his father though.

Ian looked from his father to Lira, noticing the translucence of his father's skin.

Should he pray to the Gods? What did his father mean about feeling more within himself? Ian felt boundlessly effervescent towards Lira. I will beg to make her my Queen...wait; I remember telling her she would be my Queen, and so much more. Oh the places we will go. Surely, that was when I was hurt. It was a dream. Maybe this is all a dream. Lira has just expressed that. No, this is real, Lira is real. All the rest must be as well. I am unwilling to part with any moment of the time we spent together, time that bound my soul to her soul with the kisses of passion and an eternity of promised love. I could still taste her warmed brown sugar and honey flavor. Yes, it is all too real. Atlantis is about to be torn asunder. Surely, nothing unsavory will surface, because she is delicious. I would do anything, anything at all to keep her by my side.

Just as the thought struck him, another note pierced his ears coming from the light above. He looked quickly upwards to divine the sound's origin, then moved towards his father and Lira.

"Father we must leave now! I know not nor care what you're trying to impart to me. Surely, nothing can be worth more than our loves and our loved ones lives." Ian said, gazing tenderly into Lira's eyes.

Then Ian turned to look at his father, King Minos, the most powerful man in the world besides the gods.

"Come Father." Ian said, holding out his hand. "We must be away from here now. Our lives here are over. I have somehow gained some knowledge of where I am to be. Father, you will live in a beautiful land with vast deserts and a large river called the Amazon. I will live further away with my beloved Lira."

His father turned to Ian, "You finally understand what I have been trying to unlock inside you for years, but it has been dormant until now! You see who we are. Who we are to become?"

"Yes, father, there is much that needs to be learned from all of us. We cannot take the foolhardy risk of all being in one place again. We must spread out around the world so this knowledge will not be lost. We are not truly humans, are we father?"

Minos looked at his son and then at his soon to be daughter. "No, my son, we never have been, but it is easier for mortals to accept what we have to teach that way."

Ian nodded solemnly, "I understand how that could be. I am still in awe of this room. I do not quite know what powers it or what it does, but I know it's part of me. I feel it inside my head like a low hum beyond the sounds of destruction outside. How many will be lost?"

Minos shook his head sadly, "I have no idea my son, but we must be away. Midnight is upon us."

With that, he turned away from Ian and Lira. "I am sending you to a jungle land far from here called South America. You and your bride will be beneficent rulers. As you go through this portal, you will remember the sciences, as no one has known them before. Use this knowledge and make your people prosperous and happy. You yourselves will send me fine grandchildren to rule when I am gone."

"Father," Ian said, "do not talk so. You have many good years, Sire!"

"Ian," his father looked his son in the eye. "I am far older than any structure here. Believe me when I tell you this will be the last rule I have."

He turned to Lira again. "My dear, if I have insulted you in any way, at any time, I apologize. I knew you were different when I laid eyes on you, I just did not know how vastly different. When you pass through this portal, your memories shall return with your own knowledge of what is needed."

In the distance, a loud thudding noise sounded, for all the world, like a giant tramping on their heads...tiny pings, then a loud earsplitting noise, and everything began to sway, and water was boiling close by.

King Minos hurried to the globes, moved some of the arches, and touched the glowing stones in a certain order. Suddenly, there was a whooshing sound, and the blue prismatic light from above became a doorway in the wall. King Minos gestured impatiently to the two lovers.

"Away we must be. Soon Atlantis will be no more."

Lira wistfully thought of the caress, would she ever feel it again? She had her prince, and things would be all right, wouldn't they? All of the things King Minos promised her, memories and knowledge, and she blushed thinking about babies and making them. Surely, that couldn't all be ramblings from a man who didn't resemble a man anymore. There was something just beneath the surface. She wondered to herself do I look like that. She reached up to touch her face. She felt no differently, but neither did Ian. It was the light, she thought. We are going to a jungle.

The king was getting impatient. "Hurry now, walk through. Your new world awaits you on the other side."

Ian turned and held out his hand, "Little blossom, are you with me? You may say no. You are free to leave once we walk through that door, but I cannot leave you here to die."

Lira looked up at Ian, "You are my heart. Wherever you go, I must follow, my Lord."

He smiled and said, "We are ready, father."

Ian stepped towards his father, and letting go of Lira's hand, embraced him, maybe for the last time.

"Goodbye, my Lord," he said, formally bowing to his father.

"May the gods bless you and keep you safe, my son."

As one, Lira and Prince Ian stepped through the door. It seemed like they drifted and slept, but they awoke on a beautiful white pyramid. There was jungle as far as the eye could see. It was wild, untamed, and unspeakably beautiful.

Ian said, "I think you belong here."

Lira smiled, pulling his head down for a kiss. He leaned into her.

"You still smell like warmed brown sugar and honey, may I have a taste?"

She giggled as he leaned down to lick the sweat drops from her neck to her chest. He smiled eagerly, "Still enticing, little blossom. Do you remember anything beyond Atlantis yet?"

"No, my Lord."

He arched his eyebrow again. "What is this, my Lord again? Huh? There is no one here but you and me. Would you like to be called Your Highness?"

She smiled and said saucily, "Hmm, maybe I would. Try it on me!"

He leaned very close and said, "Your Highness, would you do me the honor of letting me bathe you?"

She gasped at his suggestion, "Well, where would you be doing this at? I see no water."

He smiled, "I hear it, your highness," bowing to her.

Lira was full on laughing. He seemed so sure. After what they had been through, a bath sounded heavenly. Then she sobered as she thought of Atlantis and all the people who would never have that pleasure again.

"Please, let's bathe, Ian. We both smell like ash and worse."

He looked around, "Your wish is my command," and carried her deeper into the pyramid to find the source of the water that he heard. Down and down he went. It was getting louder. More stone steps appeared. They seemed endless. The white rock was gleaming beautifully.

CHAPTER FOURTEEN

Lira

I looked around as I was carried. I saw no signs of people. Surely, someone inhabited such an immense and glorious structure. I smelled a wonderful fresh smell. I had never smelled its equal. Lush and alive. I smelled water! Ian turned the corner. It looked as if we had walked into part of the outside. We looked upon where we stepped through the door. I could still see a white roof, the stairs, and on the opposite wall was a waterfall with beautiful flowers of orange, pink and blue, tangled in green vines hanging down from the wall. It was breathtaking. There was a pool it spilled into, perfect for bathing. Too bad we had no clean clothes, or soap. I laughed inside my own head. You have just escaped the destruction of your home, with the prince as your savior no less, and you're bemoaning clothes and soap. There are no people. Who cares what you are wearing? You silly girl! You're alive! Ian turned his head towards me and smiled as if he heard my interior dialogue.

"Would my lady care to bathe now?"

"As you wish, my Lord," I giggled as he walked over to the pool. Then he said, "Ready, little blossom?"

I smiled and shook my head, yes.

He jumped right in with both of us! I couldn't have been more surprised. I came up spluttering and shocked. The water was warm. It was lovely, and it caressed my skin. I looked for my prince, but I did not see him. I panicked and began diving beneath the water searching frantically. Maybe he hit his head! Perhaps he has bumped his head and cannot call out for aid? My mind raced with a thousand scenarios. I must rescue my prince. I came up for air and noticed an orange flower floating in the water, and behind that, a beautiful purple lily. The flowers made a path on the water, and lying lazily on the fresh aromatic moss was Ian.

I screamed, "I thought you were hurt or dead! How could you let me think that? Did you not hear me calling out for you?"

"Well, little blossom, when you came up, you floated gently out of my arms as if someone else were holding you. I thought perhaps the gods were claiming you. Did you want me to anger a god we know nothing about? Beyond that fact, you seemed to be quite enjoying the attentions. You are wonderfully clean and beautiful to behold. You look as if you belong right here."

He smiled at me, and I felt my anger dissolve away.

"My Lord, I was afraid for your life."

"Little blossom, what did I say about my Lord?"

I looked at him. He waded into the water, picked me up, and said, "You shall never have use of your feet again until you can learn to call me Ian. I think I can find some uses for your feet."

He placed me down on the emerald moss. The crushed moss smelled heavenly. He reached up and grabbed two vines, gently wrapping them around my ankles, so that my feet were apart and in the air, allowing him access to all parts of me. Since my clothes were floating in the water, I was bare to his hungry gaze.

"You are like the lovely flowers here," he said to me. "I think I will see if they complement you as well."

He picked a luscious-looking pink flower. It had a white and yellow center. He ran it along my jaw. It tickled. I reached up to knock it away, feeling embarrassed. Once again, Ian reached into the vines and gently tugged out two more to do his bidding, as if they knew what he wanted and made themselves into what he needed.

I was totally helpless to Ian and his desires in this new place. I felt a delicious ache deep inside me.

"Ian? What are you doing? This is not normal."

He smiled, "What about the last few days makes you think anything is normal?"

He ran the flower slowly down my throat.

"Do you like that, lovely one?"

Oh my gods. Do I have to answer that aloud?

He stopped and looked at me with an eyebrow raised. Apparently I did. I sighed, "Yes."

"Yes? Yes, what?"

"I like it, Ian!"

He laughed and continued the torment around my self. He stroked with the soft outer side of the flower, and then stopped at my chest.

"Do you want me to see if you like flowers elsewhere my

I gasped. *His love?*

He ran the soft flower down my stomach tickling me as he went. I thrashed against the vines. I thought they would break, but they got a little tighter. Oh, it felt good, a little more pressure somewhere. I was all feeling. Nerve endings I did not know I had came alive. I felt wetness start to spill out of me. The way I was suspended let my wetness run down, soaking my bottom as well. I had never had such intense sensations.

"Are you ready for a little more play?" Ian asked.

"Umhum...," was all I could manage.

He used the flower to gently massage my skin all around my drenched self, but never touching it directly. My insides were molten. Once again, he smiled at me as he pulled the flower back to reveal its erectness. It was surreal. I wanted him erect and inside me, but something inside me wanted to know what he was going to do next. He took the white pointed part of the flower and ran in along my lips, parting them so slightly. I could feel hot, wet drips spill out. He flicked it around until I was going out of my mind. All of the smells and feelings were too much. I began to beg..."Please, please?"

"What, little blossom?" Ian smiled.

"I need you," I said.

"Need me to what?" Ian began running the flower towards my center. I arched my hips towards him. He leaned forward to take me in his mouth. When he did, I felt his arousal against my thigh. I began to rub myself against it. He groaned. Now I would have my playtime first.

"Naughty girl," he admonished me.

He brought a beautiful yellow flower from above my head and kissed me with it in between our mouths. It tasted sweet and made me lightheaded.

I nodded enthusiastically. He smiled, "My little blossom."

I opened my mouth, and he thrust, not the whole length, but a couple inches past the head.

"Umm. Nice and slow," he said, pulling my head up by my hair.

The vines tightened again. They seemed to know what he wanted. Then he pulled my head back sharply and brought his lips down hard on mine. He began thrusting his tongue in my mouth. He tasted so good. I couldn't help but get wetter. Which of us was so enticing, or was it the mingling taste of us both?

He rose and walked around me a couple times. I was feeling very exposed by then. Just as he said, "I have never seen anything so lovely..." I felt a brush against my neck, a light sensation that followed with a hot breath. I looked around, nothing. I was still lightheaded; maybe I imagined it.

"Let's see if the flower complements you."

With that remark, he took one long slow lick inward. I began to raise my hips towards him when his tongue came out and licked a line upwards to my from belly to neck. I have never felt anything as intense as that moment. I thought I could hang suspended for eternity as long as he kept up those lashing strokes. I was straining towards something, then he moved his other hand. He held me up with one hand, and began making heat inside me, and running his other finger down to my back. It hurt in a glorious kind of way. I wanted something else so I moved to the side a bit.

Ian looked up at me. "Yes, my love?"

I blushed furiously. "I need something more!"

He smiled and began massaging. I jumped. I started to feel not so excited. Just then, a hot breath across my body distracted me. Umm. That felt nice.

I thought it must be the heat, because it was very hot. My gods, again? Did the caress travel with me even here? I gave in completely.

Ian rose above me. "Are you ready, little blossom?"

"Oh, oh...yes."

Yes, to whatever. I was so hot inside. I thought I was feverish.

I opened my eyes wide and saw Ian straining and sweating to hold back. I knew I was a virgin except for what we had done previously, but was that right?

"Woman, you unman me. Hold still."

I tried, but hot breath was on my clit. My womanhood ached to clench around him. Even my womb felt like it was clenching. Slowly, ever so slowly, he began to rock inside me. I was fighting to attain something. I moved towards something earth shattering.

Ian pulled away and moved back towards me with heat. The vines were swinging to help him on each swing. I was just along for the ride. What an unbelievable ride it was. I felt little patters of something on my chest. I wanted to look, but I did not. I looked at Ian instead. His eyes were glowing blue again. As he pumped deep, I felt a quaking begin inside me as if I had my own Atlantis there. Would I be torn apart as well?

Ian increased his pace and began fingering the flower as I swung back towards him. The vines were doing a lot of the work. He began to shudder.

"Come to me little blossom! Let me see you bloom for me."

Oh, that was like a magic button that released the dam. I knew I was a sweating mess, but whatever happened, I never wanted it to end. Ian collapsed on top of me. I was not sure what to do. I laughed to myself. This would be when we find people. I was strung up like an offering to the gods, and lay there with a god collapsed on top of me. I began to giggle again. Ian cracked an eye and peered at me.

"My love, do you find my lovemaking humorous?"

"No, Ian," I hurried to reply. "I was imagining what the local people would think if they met us like this."

Ian looked down and laughed. "Well surely, with you strung up, covered in flowers and dew, you are a goddess."

"I must be your consort at least. Do you not agree? Ian you tease me. Let me down now, please my Lord." I said sarcastically.

"Ah, there's that fire I have been looking for, unexpected though it is at the moment. You are a ravishing sight. I wish to have one last look to commit to memory before I let you down, my love."

"Ian, do you tell every woman you have tied up that you love her?"

"Little blossom, I have never told a single woman in my life I loved her."

He began to loosen the vines on me, which seemed to melt away at his touch. I had not a mark on me. Remarkable, I thought.

"Wait. You have never said that to ANY woman?"

"No, I have not, not even in jest."

"Why are you saying it to me? You barely know me. I will be with you without the words. I do not lie! I am not little blossom. I love you."

I turned to him and took his hand in mine.

"I love you with all my heart, Ian. Anything you want from me is yours."

He smiled, "Do not tempt me woman! You look enticing enough for any man or god. Now let us wash again and see if we can find some food and then some people."

We walked hand in hand, as if we were the first man and woman on earth, as naked as we were born. We stepped into the exquisite warmth, the water lapping against our legs as we sank down onto the natural stone ledge.

"Ah," I murmured, "this is heavenly."

Ian could not agree more so he chose not to voice it. He reached over and pulled me into his lap.

"I love you," he said quietly, as he wrapped his arms around me contentedly.

I leaned back looking up at him. "You just love me because I am the only woman here."

He looked down at me lovingly. "No, little blossom. From the moment I set eyes upon you, I loved you."

I squinted at him, which made him laugh and push me away.

"Do you mock me woman?" he demanded.

"No, I am trying to see if you have been struck blind or have some other trauma."

He began to splash me. "I will show you trauma!"

"My Lord, show pity," I cried.

"Are you hurt?" He immediately quit moving. It was very humid and almost foggy in the grotto.

I popped up behind him and covered his eyes. "Now do you love me?" I asked.

"Of course you vixen, but you still call me my Lord! Penalties shall be forthcoming!"

He pulled me over his shoulder and across his knees in one movement. He began to lightly swat my bottom. Every word he punctuated with a slap. "You will no longer call me my Lord."

"No, please stop!"

"Are you sure?" he asked.

"Yes, yes, Ian." He assessed our position, as he was getting a little uncomfortable in his region in contact with my belly and wet curls. The water was soothing.

Ian said, "I think you should prove it to me."

I looked back at him questionably. "How am I to do that I A N?"

He grinned at me drawing out his name.

"Turn around and face me on your knees," he said.

I obediently did, looking up at him, with water almost to my neck.

He smiled, "Your hair is floating about you. You look like a goddess."

I smiled shyly, "Thank you."

Ian said, "Lean forward, little blossom. Take me in your mouth."

CHAPTER FIFTEEN

Prince Ian
He could feel her against him. He thought he would lose himself right then. She drives me crazy, he thought to himself. He leaned back, somewhat out of the water.

"Like that Ian?" she asked sweetly. She ran her tongue down the length and back up slowly, so slowly. He was about to push her head down on him, when she began to take him in. The feeling was indescribable. It was near reverence for him. The Gods had gifted him greatly. He hoped to always be worthy of it. He was himself in and out of her mouth.. He erupted like the volcanic cloud of Atlantis. A little dribbled down her chin. He loved the look of pearlescence against her lovely tan skin. He brought her up against him. Lira locked her legs around his back. He smothered her face and neck with kisses.

She laughed. "That is my compensation for almost drowning!"

He laughed even harder. "You never would have drowned. You can stand up in this water."

She looked at him. "That is not the kind of drowning I meant."

"Lira? Are you angry I want you so much?"

"No, I am not angry! You're a beast is all."

"What? I am a considerate beast surely!"

"No, you spanked me, tried to drown me two ways, and I'm sore in places," she stammered, "and I'm hungry. Pouting now."

Ian said, "I am sorry you have been misused. Let us find our clothes and some food."

Lira peered up at him, "Really this time?"

"By, The Gods wench! Yes, really this time!"

He smiled and got out of the water, pulling her up with him. Their clothes had floated onto some beautiful water lilies. Miraculously, they were dry and smelled heavenly. They dressed in silence, both wondering what they would find.

CHAPTER SIXTEEN

Prince Ian & Lira
As one, they ascended towards the steps, then heard a loud caw. A beautiful brightly colored bird flew by them up the stairs as if to show the way. They looked at each other and began to follow.

Lira said, "The stairs seemed less on the way down."

He lifted her up and began carrying her.

"Will you carry me the rest of my life?"

"As long as you will let me, little blossom. Having you in my arms is a joy I would not forgo."

They reached the top of the temple. Walking out into the sunshine, they were once again struck by the beauty that surrounded them, but no lake, no river.

"I think I see the sparkle of water to the side of us in the distance," Ian said. "I guess the people have deserted this place? I wonder why my father sent us here. There is no one. I have no idea what to do."

Lira smiled, "We're together. We will figure it out. Let us walk and see what there is to see."

He laughed, "More steps? Would you be carried?"

"No, I have no desire to fall down this huge stone pyramid Ian."

"Onward then."

They reached the bottom. The trees, flowers, and vines were huge and tangled from the ground view, and further away, there were smaller pyramids. They headed that way and came upon a huge white circular stone with engravings of people with hats. What looked like a bird, flew overhead. As they walked around the stone, they realized it was only partially inscribed.

"It is amazing." Lira murmured.

"Indeed, great skill was used here. But where are the people?" Ian headed further down what looked like a well-worn path and saw grass-covered platforms with big palm fronds. Fruits and vegetables were there, some not known, and an animal he did not recognize had been smoked. Canteens were hanging from the ceiling. He called out,

"Hello? Hello? We are friends! We are unarmed! We came from the temple."

A small, delicate looking woman came from the forest, bowing and gesturing towards the food.

"Dear lady, please tell us where we are." Ian asked.

"You are the gods? We saw the prophesied blue fire streak across the sky and land in the temple. We have kept faith all these years you would return. This feast is in your honor. The people would see you when you are refreshed enough to do so?"

"Yes. Your name, dear lady?"

"I am Needa."

"I am Ian, and this is my Lady, Lira."

She bowed. "I am honored. Should you need anything just call out. I will get proper robes for you both."

They looked at each other. Indeed, they looked ragged.

"Thank you, Needa. New robes would be welcomed."

She scurried off.

Ian smiled. "You are hungry, little blossom?"

"Well, yes, but this is enough to feed a village."

"Don't look a gift bird in the mouth," he retorted.

As he sat, he grabbed a beautifully made wooden bowl and began filling it with dates, oranges, cherries, cucumbers, and tomatoes. He stood and grabbed the flagon, pouring out a sweet smelling wine. He tasted it. It was very good.

"Lira, try some my love."

She sat next to him and ate whatever he ate first, and proclaimed it good. They dozed a while in the heat. Both awoke famished again. Ian cut up some of the meat.

"Delicious," he declared. "Tastes like the bull from home," he said, with a look that pained him.

She reached up and touched his face. "We will all miss home. We were sent here to make a new home."

"Yes, by the gods, we shall. We will be married and start our own dynasty."

She laughed, "Are you so sure then?"

"Well, yes, what else would we do?" Ian asked.

"Well, maybe you might try asking me first."

"Oh, that game, is it? Do you want to marry me, Lira?"

"Now, that is not really asking, is it?" Lira said.

"Of course it is," Ian scoffed.

She shook her head, "Less talking, more eating," then she promptly shoved meat in his surprised mouth. Needa came back with beautiful blue and silver lightweight robes that draped from the shoulder, and lovely bracelets and necklaces of a light blue and black cracked color, with rainbows shooting through some of them. She also brought a younger man. She introduced him as her son, Slade. He was the leader of the clan there and wanted to welcome their new gods.

Lira said, "We are not gods."

Needa raised an eyebrow.

Ian said, "How would you explain how we got here and the prophecy?"

Lira remembered what had happened in Atlantis. She was not sure that Ian and his father were not gods. In truth, after what she had seen, that might very well be.

When they were dressed, fed, and rested, Slade came to make an offering to them. It was the beautiful bird from the temple. He meant to cut its throat over the rock!

"No, please do not do this." Lira pleaded. "It is beautiful. Letting it live will honor us more."

Ian looked at her, but said nothing. Slade looked up, "As you will it. What would you like? I can tether him, cage him, or free him."

"A light tether and a nice perch. That would be perfect."

"As you command, my Lady."

Ian smiled and said, "Soft spot already?"

She said, "Mayhap, this is a god in disguise come to test us? It could be; we are in a new place. It never hurts to err on the side of caution. Yet I would not want to offend our subjects already. Surely there is another compromise."

"Yes," Ian said, "I will talk with Needa."

He stepped out from the lovely cool hut. Immediately, Needa emerged as if waiting for his summons.

"How can I serve you, my Lord?"

"I would like to have a conversation with you, an honest, open one."

"Yes," she looked at Ian.

"I wonder what your people's expectations are. I would know some of your history, so I may better help us all."

Lira swelled with pride. This was not the spoiled prince she had met. He had truly changed.

Needa, said, "However I can help. "

"Let's see Slade with where your gods live."

"In the temple where you arrived, my Lord."

"Alright, do your gods require sacrifices?"

"Yes, usually human blood sacrifices, but not death unless a punishment is warranted. We also use beautiful things as tribute."

Ian said, "I see no village, no city. Where does the line of the empire end?"

"Many days walk from here. There is a village beyond the trees closer to the water of the gods."

He looked at Lira. "The water I told you I had seen earlier."

"Very good. I will visit the village in a day or so. At the temple there are no furnishings but carved rock."

"Yes, my Lord, we wait for you to decide if you would have thrones or cushions indoors."

"We would like to be accessible to all, so both."

She nodded her head. "We will bring all our Lord's needs before you leave here."

"I would appreciate that, Needa, would you continue to advise me?"

"If it is your will, my Lord."

"It is," Ian said firmly. "I will retire for now and ponder what you have told me."

Lira watched all this quietly. What a difference a Midnight could make.

Ian returned to Lira's side, "What do you think, my love?" Ian asked her.

"I think we need to be cautious and worthy," she replied.

"Spoken like a true leader. We shall be."

He took her hand, turning it back and forth. She looked at him, "What is it?"

"Nothing, my love. I would adorn these lovely hands with all manner of jewels. But

I can think of none that would match your eyes."

"Ian, you're making me blush and it's so hot out here."

"Did I hear you're getting hot? I know a remedy for that." He ran his hand up her robe towards her core.

"No, not right here where everyone can see!"

Laughing, he said, "Fine, we do not want to embarrass anyone, do we?"

He laid down and pulled her into his side, and before long, they were sound asleep.

CHAPTER SEVENTEEN

Prince Ian

Ian came awake with a start. Oh, it was all a dream. He was back in Atlantis and should be happy, but instead Ian felt desolate. All the people were safe...his father, his country, but what a lovely dream it was.

He stretched and grabbed a glass of wine. Looked out at his gleaming city of gold and white marble with topaz blue waters, Ian decided to speak with his father about this strange dream. Mayhap the oracles could divine some things for him. He headed down to the throne room.

It was strange no one was there, no counselors no supplicants. He headed down the stairs towards the kitchen. There was a room back there in his dream. There was no one in the kitchen either. It was as if the palace was abandoned. Why was he not awakened?

Something was seriously amiss! Ian began to panic!

Racing downstairs, he looked for the invisible hollow spot to enter a room that shouldn't be there. Still he felt he must find it. He walked slowly along the wall, knocking occasionally. Clunk, clunk. Tap, tap. Ah. He pressed and the wall moved stealthily inwards.

"Father?"

No reply. There were the books, the miniature of the city, and as he looked up, he saw the blue glow. It wasn't quite the strobing effect it was before, but a prismatic blue glow falling upon everything. The rotating metal globes are intact. How strange, he thought with a strong sense of something. Something urgent.

Where is Lira? He ran out of the chamber yelling her name!

"Is anyone here?"

The curtains were a billowing white cloud off the southern veranda. Ian spotted a ship, but it was so far away. That meant there were people about. Perhaps everyone left the palace because of the disease. Maybe Lira went with them. She was immune. What about the nights together, surely that was not just a dream? He could taste the food, the air, and her. He decided to locate the oracle and find out what happened.

I told her she would be my queen. I told her I loved her. Wait. She never told me she loved me! Not once! As I sat down on the step dumbstruck, I relived what I had done, what I had dreamed. *Now I look at what is in front of me. Surely, this is the God's' punishment for my offending them. No one could endure the loss of so much, to be given so much in the blink of an eye. There is a lesson here. When I figure that out, my life will return to normal. Normal? What is that? I can find no one about. My father missing, as is Lira. I have no idea what is happening. The dream seemed real, but I am in Atlantis. It is unharmed. No eruptions, no flooding, no destruction whatsoever. Also, no people. It is as quiet as a grave as if no person has been here at all. I am truly puzzled. Where do I go from here?*

CHAPTER EIGHTEEN

Lira

What a beautiful place we had come to. Everything was pleasing to me after the horrific destruction of Atlantis. What a refreshing nap. I saw that everything was still lovely. There was my bird on his perch, multicolored plumes waving in the breeze. Where was Ian? Mayhap he went to the village with Needa. Surely, he would have let me to know he was leaving. Well, maybe he wanted to let me rest. Very sweet of him. I decided to take a walk and explore a little.

As I stepped down, the bird cawed once, twice.

I looked at the bird. "Are you in truth a guide? Are you telling me to stay here? Should I not look about a bit?"

Just then, Needa stepped out from the forest. "My Lady? How can I serve you?"

"Needa, can you tell me where Lord Ian is?"

She raised an eyebrow, "My Lady, I have no idea."

"What? Could he be with your son?"

"No, my Lady. He was here with you."

"Enough my Lady stuff. I am no more than you."

Needa bowed to me. "As you wish."

"No, it is truth. Call me Lira." I said. "Now, how do I find Lord Ian?"

"I have no clue, Lira," she murmured. "How do you track a god? I have no arts for such."

I began to panic. "Could you ask your son to organize search parties and look for him?"

"I will go quickly now. Will you be well on your own?"

"I am fine. Aren't I safe here?"

"As safe as royalty unknown can be, I expect." Needa answered with brutal honesty.

"What do you mean?" I asked. "I am not royalty. I have just explained that to you."

"As you say." Needa agreed. "But you came here from the temple on a blue light that lit up the sky for all to see. The temple is for Gods and royalty."

"I see the misunderstanding, but I simply traveled with Lord Ian."

"As you say," Needa agreed amicably.

"None of this matters. Let us find Ian with all haste, please."

Needa said, "I will go to the village and find my son and tell him what is needed. I will return quickly. Call out if you need anything, or let the bird off the tether. He will find his way to me."

I looked at the bird again with suspicion. "Alright, please hurry! I have a feeling he is in need, if not in danger."

I felt dread in the pit of my stomach, worse than when Atlantis was being destroyed! What could have happened? Nothing had disturbed my sleep. Where was he? I knew these past few days had been too good to be true. No one could change that much in so little a time. Saying he would make me his queen. He even said he loved me. I could not say it back. He was too good for me. Something happened to people I loved. They died or disappeared. I could not ruin such a beautiful feeling between Ian and me. I did not want it to end. The moment I let my guard down and began to think it could be real, that it could happen, he disappeared as if he never was.

"Gods, don't take everything from me again." I wailed. "I need him. Truly."

The bird made a high-pitched warble. Slade and four men came out of the woods from behind her. They were so quiet.

"Can you find my Lord Ian?"

Slade inclined his head. "We have looked all around the hut. There are no footprints anywhere. Needa is the only one to have a recent print. Perhaps he has returned home on his blue light."

"No, it's not possible!" I cried. "Our home was destroyed around us even as we came here. There is nothing to return to! Can you check the temple?"

"No, my Lady. We may not go inside unless accompanied by a god or goddess like yourself."

I began stalking towards the hut edge. The bird let out a loud caw.

"Alright, you can come too!"

I let the bird off the tether. He aimed straight and true for the pyramid. As it came fully into view, I gasped. It was even bigger than I remembered. Surely, gods lived there. Who else would need that big of a place?

Needa, in step behind her, heard the gasp as they came upon the pyramid.

"My Lady? Are you well?"

"Why yes. I didn't remember the immensity of the temple, and I am so very worried about our Lord Ian. Let us hasten on now."

Slade led the way again.

There were no signs that anyone had been that way. Why would Ian leave me like that? There must be something wrong? He was so patient, tender, and loving with me. Would he abandon me here as I was abandoned as a child? Was there something wrong with me? A thousand other thoughts ran through my mind. He has to be ok!

We were finally at the steps of the great white pyramid with its massive stairs that rose to the sky. The gods or protectors at the base of it looked like feathered lizards. They were very intimidating indeed. I shrank away from the open mouth of one head that easily took up half my body size.

Slade bowed to the Godhead and said ,Quetzal, looking at me quizzically. I quickly glanced at Needa who inclined her head. She looked back at Slade. I bowed to the statue as well. Slade seemed satisfied with the walk along the giant pyramid. There was still no sign of Ian; I worried.

After an exhaustive walk around the temple, we returned to the statue of Quetzal. At this point, I was exhausted. Needa stepped up. "Would you like refreshment my Lady?"

"Oh, that would be lovely," I exclaimed in relief.

Needa smiled and clapped her hands. Some of the villagers laid down a portable hut floor, some pillows, and a small table with various fruits I didn't recognize, and thank the gods, wine! They erected a small roof to shade me, made of tree boughs. It really was quite lovely. It would be perfect if I could find Ian.

The bird flew around after his handler set up his perch and lengthened his tether, which looked like the smallest gold chain. I smiled as I thought of the bird being some sort of guide. I was very glad I did not let them sacrifice it. The heat of the day was beginning to dissipate somewhat. What a relief.

"Needa, I must look in the temple for my Lord Ian."

Needa looked at me and up into the sky for a few moments.

"As you will, my Lady."

I rose from my comfortable resting place and turned to the bird's tether. For some reason, I knew this was important. Letting the gold chain dangle lightly in my hand, I let him loose to fly. *Be safe and bring my Lord Ian to me,* I thought silently.

Immediately, the bird began circling the stairs ahead of me. I ascended the stairs, following the bird, that seemed to be my guide. It was a very arduous task, seeming to ascend straight to the heavens. I sat for a moment, everyone else below me doing the same.

Well, he must be up here. I could see half the land, but no sign of anything. As I looked around at the beautiful, unending landscape of jungle, I caught sight of water just like Ian said. The refraction from the light was like a beacon. Mayhap somehow, Ian had found a way to access the room that was in Atlantis. It almost looked like the same prismatic effect as the room we were in before. I felt something inside me, a warm feeling, then a soft gentle caress across my shoulders. *Is the caress back*, I thought excitedly? Maybe I was not alone here. Then, I felt a tickle at my side. That felt so much better.

"Hurry," I turned to Needa. "We must get to the top! I must see the water!"

Needa looked befuddled. "What water my Lady?"

I pointed to the south. "There. I see the light glinting off the water."

Needa looked at me and said, "My Lady, do you speak of the sacred Cenotes?"

"What does that mean?" I asked.

"Our gods live in the sacred Cenotes. We guard their privacy. The gods have a regular festival and sacrifice there. Do you not have Cenotes where you come from?"

Slade immediately cleared his throat and went down on one knee. "My mother meant no offense. Please forgive her. Of course you know where the gods live, you are one."

I looked from mother to son, trying to figure out a correct response. I did not have Ian's surety. I was not born into royalty and had no idea who I was. Another cool caress lifted my hair off my shoulders. To the natives, I was a frightening and beautiful god. It looked like blue lightning was lifting my mahogany hair around my head. They all fell to their knees, heads bowed. I looked down at them.

"Please get up; we must go to the top of the temple. I have an extreme need to see the land and find Lord Ian."

Needa stood up. "As you wish, my Lady," handing her the golden tether.

The bird, beautiful and multicolored with a long blue tail feather, swept by, the feather caressing my face lightly. Up the steep white steps we climbed, and I knew something was about to happen. I could feel it in my stomach. In my mind, it was a night lily about to unfurl for the moon's glow. As I thought more and more about the glow, I refocused my eyes on the water to the south. He had to be there where the water was. Right? I asked the bird, Quetzal. The bird squawked, and flew around my head.

I thought quickly. I felt that time was growing short for Ian. I had to help him somehow. Where could he have gone? And for what reason?

I looked at Needa, "Is there any reason for our Lord to have journeyed to the water?"

"No, my Lady, unless he was of a mind to make sacrifices or commune with the gods, but surely, he would have us guide him in this endeavor? I cannot pretend to know a god's mind though, my Lady. Maybe he shifted to a blue ray of light once more and will return to the temple once he has his answers."

"Well, someone better have some answers soon!" I said, exasperated. My worry for Ian was making me short-tempered, and I did not want to take that out on Needa.

"I apologize Needa." I took her hands. "My worry for my Lord has gotten the best of me. I should not have lashed out at you. I am sorry."

Needa squeezed my hands in return. "My Lady, there is no need to apologize. You awoke with our Lord gone. I would feel panic if my loved ones were gone. God or no. I appreciate your honesty. It is my honor to serve one such as you. I am happy to know you put the needs of others above yourself. You will be a great ruler."

I looked down, "I have no rights to rule. I am a servant to my Lord in truth."

Needa smiled, "Aren't we all servants to someone my Lady? You do not need royal blood to be royalty. If the Gods will it, so will it be. You stand at the al

Slade of the greatest temple we know. No man, woman, or child comes here without a price. You are unscathed, and being in your presence, so are we. That is all the proof I need."

Slade came back into the chamber. "My Lady we have found no sign of anyone alone here. There are two tracks. What can I do to serve?"

"Slade, you have been a great help to me and my Lord Ian. When he returns, he will reward you himself. For now, can you find us some food and drink? I am parched and starving all of a sudden."

Quetzal flew around the room and landed on a stone. It was a throne to be exact. It glowed green in spots. There were letters, but I couldn't read them. I asked Needa what it said.

"I am sorry my Lady, that is the god's writing. I know not what it says."

She looked down, crestfallen.

"Needa?" I asked in an inquiring tone, "Would you serve me faithfully if I were not from here, not a god?"

"My Lady," Needa replied. "I did see you come in on a bolt of blue light with our Lord Ian. I also saw the same blue light dancing in your hair just now. Yes, I will serve you no matter what. On my honor."

I was startled. Blue light in my hair? I felt nothing. I pulled my hair around and saw nothing. I looked over at Quetzal.

"Beautiful bird, can you show me where my Lord has gone? I will free you and follow you hither."

The bird arched its abnormally long tail feather. Surely, it was the most beautiful bird I had ever seen.

As if it heard me, Quetzal let out a trilling noise. The men appeared shaken and looked about for an attack. I walked over to Quetzal, running my hand down his head and his tail.

"I beseech you, my lovely one. Please help me find my...I almost said love...my Lord."

The bird looked me straight in the eye and flew back into the temple. I jumped up, running after Quetzal. Everyone parted, then followed. He was heading further into the temple, back where we had come from in the beginning. My cheeks heated at the thoughts of what had transpired there just about a day ago. How did I let Ian inside my soul in that short of a time? I had vowed never to love anyone again! Love got people killed or worse; missing. However, when I arrived in Atlantis, I had no doubt I was alone, because I had loved someone, even if I was just a child. As I grew, I became more certain that I was cursed. Ian was caught in my curse because I had let my guard down. I let him in, but how could I deny what was between us? He left me no choice when he made my body respond like that. Oh, how I missed him.

CHAPTER NINETEEN

Prince Ian
  I have wandered right out of my mind it appears. I am in a ghost Atlantis. There is literally no one here. All the furnishings are here. Everything is untouched as if everyone is out for a stroll along the seashore, and somehow, I am caught. How can I find my way back to Lira, when my lovely city is destroyed by the gods in a fit of rage? Man has never seen such destruction...fire from the earth erupting like the tales of dragons, whole farms swallowed up as if a giant cyclops got hungry. Then the shaking as if Zeus himself rattled the walls. Next, the walls of water, a hundred feet high, smashing through the outer walls. As the water met with the fire, steam poured out. Did Zeus and Poseidon battle for control of Atlantis? That would explain the hurling of rocks as big as homes; the shaking of the palace. The oracles said Atlantis would be gone in a day. If that is true, how am I standing here looking at a perfect azure blue ocean? I do not understand. I can find no living thing.

  As he contemplated for a few moments, something tickled his thoughts, but he couldn't quite grasp it. The last time he had looked at this sky, there was no sky, but an inferno of smoke, fire, and steaming clouds that blotted out the heavens except for the thunderbolts Zeus hurled throughout. Ian remembered the palace walls falling in. He also remembered the most magical night of his life with Lira. He was getting hard thinking about her, calling to mind her beautiful mahogany hair with a few blonde lights, those soul piercing violet eyes that darkened to almost sapphire blue when she was aroused, the tan, soft skin. Her perfect bosomss were ripe and inviting. Lower, a lovely curved stomach that led to lush full hips, and the warmed brown sugar and honey taste of her, his little blossom which he had deflowered. He could not help but feel bereft without her presence. From the moment he had laid eyes on her in the throne room, he knew he was lost. He would love her until the day he died.

Wait. Had he indeed died? Is that what happened here? Is this his Elysian Fields? If so, where were all his loved ones? Surely, he had not earned a trip to tartarus. He did not truly want to be alone even if that's what he had told his father. He just did not want to rush into a marriage with someone he did not like, much less love.

Ian thought, *was this a punishment for not doing my duty by my father and my kingdom? To find love and in the same night have my beloved city torn away as well? Now I am condemned to wander here a ghost to what might have been.*

Ian, feeling more and more melancholy, found his way back to his rooms. All was as it had been...the food, dates, figs, luscious grapes, mulled, spiced wine, and the smell of her... Lira. He sat down in the nest of pillows where they had made mind blowing, fantastic love, the kind you hear about and scoff, but it was true, heartbreakingly so. The thought that he would never taste those lips again or cup those luscious ass cheeks as she rode him, made him groan in despair. The gods had been truly cruel to give him such a gift, only to take it so quickly. Maybe he had a lesson to learn in this and all would be well. The priests talked of the gods playing at such games for their amusement and humans' benefit of learning. What lesson could he learn? He was too prideful. He did not obey his father. Nothing he could think of. He began to pray to every deity.

Please return me to Lira. I promise to be worthy of her and worship you in every thought and deed. I regret failing my city. I would gladly beg for another chance to be the prince that my people deserve. I could not ask for anything great, my gods and goddesses.

Ian listened so hard, but all he heard was the sound of his own heart beating. Not even wind stirred to ease his torment. If he could take back hurting Lira in any way, he would. Thinking about her, there was an otherworldly quality there. Never had he come across a beauty such as hers. She was surely the offspring of a god or goddess. She was too perfect. Was that the test? Then he failed. He loved her truly and desperately. The more he thought about it the worse he felt.

We left. My father left. Is he in Egypt now? Can I take a boat there and find out what happened? I can manage a small boat on my own. I am a prince, not a small child.

Ian began to gather provisions for what he thought to be three days at sea. He set about looking through the assembled boats in the first ring harbor, then wondered how it would work. There were no guards to open the gates of each ring.

Ian heard a noise and whipped around. Just a few feet from him sat Lira's bird, Quetzal. He rubbed his eyes, but it still sat there looking at him as if waiting for something. Was Lira hurt? What in the world was the bird doing there? How did it arrive from so far away? The bird circled him, and as it did, the long blue tail feather caressed his face. He almost felt serene for a moment.

"Quetzal, can you take me to Lira?"

He could not believe he just asked a bird for help! Nevertheless, he needed help. There could not be that many of this kind of bird. Lira saved it thinking it was a test from the local gods. Perhaps it was a test, and his Lira passed with flying colors. Now, to find a way back to her.

Quetzal cawed again and took flight in the same way as he had arrived. Perhaps this was a good omen! Ian got in the boat, packing everything and strapping it down. There was no wind so he began rowing. That was truly some humbling work. At each guard's station, Ian tied up the boat and operated the tower, always on the lookout for life, but alas, there was none. The bird had disappeared.

That is OK, Ian thought. *I think that means Lira is alive and searching for me.*

He hoped and he prayed. He opened the last gate leading from Atlantis. He looked back at the great city, gleaming white and gold, casting shadows on the water. He turned his attention to the sea and finding his father. His father would know how to find Lira. He had to; after all, he sent them there.

As he lay in the boat drifting, he looked up at the clouds and thought some looked much like her face.Oh, it was pure torture. He sat up and began to row the boat again.

The sooner I get there, the faster I can take her in my arms and never let her go. I will marry her and make her Queen. She will be adorned in jewels and beautiful silk gowns.

His mouth watered at the thought of taking the gowns off slowly until he revealed each lovely, piece, kissing his way down as each inch was displayed. He could not stand the thought of her in danger or not being by his side.

I must get to Egypt and find out how to get back to her. I cannot make the room work that we were in. Therefore, my father must have had means to travel when he was not in Atlantis. He must have used the door of blue light himself. God's willing it can be used to send me back to Lira.

He thought of a jungle and a giant white pyramid with a hot spring grotto at the center of it in the bottom half. Beautiful and restful once the fun was over. He could never have dreamed of a better setting in which to make love to his little blossom. He laid the oar down and stretched out over the bench, and pondering his life, falling into a deep sleep, lulled by the rocking of the boat.

CHAPTER TWENTY

L**ira**
    Lira had followed Quetzal to the grotto. She was sitting on the side of the pool, letting her feet dangle into the lovely warm water that seemed to caress her feet. Quetzal circled once more, his long blue feather caressing her face and when she blinked, he was gone. She was not sure she had seen that, but he was not there. He was gone just like Ian. Was it something similar to what brought her and Ian? Did the bird know that way to travel? Surely, he must be a messenger from the Gods, or a God himself in disguise. What fortune she did not have him killed! She was feeling quite alone now. She stood and sat on the ledge hugging her knees to her chest. *Please be ok Ian! Please!*

She sat there for hours until Needa called down. "My Lady? We have food and drink prepared."

She had totally forgotten she requested a meal, but as her stomach was growling, it apparently had not forgotten.

"I am coming Needa," she called.

Lira hoped by leaving the grotto, nothing would happen in the meantime. She did not want to miss a chance to bring back Ian.

The spread before her looked fit for a hall full of gods. There was deer, fish, turkey, and some yellow vegetable with tiny buds on it. There was an orange vegetable similar to a sweet potato and mouthwatering desserts...cinnamon and sugar covering a bread like substance. Watermelon, various other fruits and dips, and tea and cocoa were there and a salad with tomatoes and peppers.

She began eating the salad. Oh gods, her mouth and throat were on fire. She could not breathe. She was sweating. Maybe they poisoned her food.

Needa, seeing her distress, came over with a small bowl filled with opalescent liquid and told her to drink. She did not question. She just drank. It was slightly bitter but eased the burning all the way to her stomach. What in the gods name was that? Lira nearly yelled.

Needa asked, "The drink my lady?"

"Yes and the salad! Are you trying to kill me? If so, I prefer I knife or an axe. Less painful."

Needa looked like she was about to laugh when Lira raised an eyebrow.

"My Lady, no harm was meant. This is the normal salad here. Habanero and jalapeño, ghost peppers, turnips, lettuce, tomato, and goat cheese. The lemonade aids in neutralizing the burn. We had no idea you had such sensitivity. We will be more careful in the future."

Lira looked at her. "I appreciate all the effort you expended. I just had no idea what a bad burning sensation there was. Could you point more towards the dishes that are less umm, fiery?"

Needa smiled, "Of course."

She filled a bowl with turkey and deer and another with vegetables with a side of cheese sauce. Lira ate with gusto.

"This is magnificent. I appreciate all your work. Please share amongst yourselves."

Needa nodded to Slade. The men came with bowls and picked assorted dishes. All seemed to favor the salad. Twilight was approaching, and Lira was getting to the point of exhaustion.

Needa looked at her mistress, "Are you tired my Lady?"

"Yes, I am afraid tired does not do it justice."

Needa smiled, "I will ready you a sleeping chamber."

"That would be amazing if you could. Thank you for everything."

"My duty, my Lady"

Lira yawned again. Soon after, Needa returned.

"Your room has been made ready my Lady. If you would follow me."

Quetzal returned from out of nowhere. The bird looked at her quizzically and flew on ahead where it looked like the temple ended. Needa pushed on the torch lamp and a huge rock turned seamlessly inward.

"This is your room. None may pass its walls except the Lord and yourself till you rise in the morning."

Quetzal was making himself at home perched atop a four-poster bed, white and green with vines and a white type of netting. Needa explained it was to keep bugs out.

"Oh, that makes sense," Lira said. "How are bugs going to get me when the wall is a perfect fit?"

Needa smiled. "We opened the door, did we not? If our Lord comes home, he will open the door too. There is a sickness you can get from bugs here, a very bad one. Many people die."

Lira thought that over. "Where I am from, there was a great sickness and too many died, but I was immune."

"That is good to hear," Needa replied. "You sound more like a god every time you speak."

Lira laid down. Needa said, "If there is nothing else, I will take my leave now. We will camp at the bottom of the temple. If you have a need, please yell, my Lady."

"That is agreeable. Goodnight, Needa."

"Goodnight, my Lady," Needa replied.

As Lira went to sleep, she dreamed of vines, flowers, and a man she lost and hoped to see soon.

She awoke to a soft caressing breeze across her face. She stretched and slowly opened her eyes. She was in a beautiful white stone room with characters painted in vivid colors. An almost transparent white netting surrounding her bed of raised pillows with a satin cover in a turquoise blue. She felt the breeze again. Did Needa not say not even a bug could get in without her opening the door. Had Ian returned? She sat up immediately; hope blossoming in her chest at the thought of seeing her prince again. The feel of his arms around her.

"Ian," she called out. No reply greeted her. She felt a hug around her shoulders. She looked around wildly for its source. No one. Then a soft brush against her cheek as if in reassurance. It was the caress! It had somehow found her again. Mayhap it never left her. She arose and shook out her hair and straightened her clothing. Looking down at the lovely blue and gold gauze robe, it felt comforting as well. It was time to sSladet looking for Ian again.

She gazed at the vivid characters. She walked to the wall and looked at them closely. She gasped. There was Quetzal, her bird, and a copy of the globes that were on the wall in Atlantis. How could that be?

As she paced, she looked about. The room was glowing a soft blue and light green. Where was the light coming from? She could find no source for it. Walking behind the bed, she felt faint. The picture there was of King Minos as he looked the night they left Atlantis...tall, blonde, with glowing blue eyes that had projected inhuman power and intelligence. Ian himself had also looked like that. Perhaps they are together somewhere, she thought. Mayhap Ian had gone back to see what had happened to his father and his people, but why leave her here?

As thoughts tumbled chaotically through her mind, she kept coming back to maybe he did not want her and left her there. She really did not belong anywhere.

Again the caress across her shoulders. *Can you talk to me? Do you have a name? More importantly, do you have any answers? I could really use some right now.* Nothing. Why would she expect anything else? She sighed and walked to the giant stone door. With a gentle nudge, it opened. She marveled at the sheer size of it. A couple of tons at least. When it closed, she could not even see a seam. Again, the similarities to the room in Atlantis struck her.

As she neared the stairs, Needa appeared. "My Lady? Did you have a restful sleep?" Needa asked, bowing to her.

"Yes, I did, I feel quite refreshed actually. Also very curious. Has there been any word of our Lord Ian?"

"No, my Lady," Needa shook her head regretfully. "I had hoped you would awaken with him beside you."

Lira responded, "As did I. Needa?"

"Yes, my Lady?" Needa replied.

"There are paintings or perhaps painted carvings in my room. Do you know what they mean or who put them there?"

"No, my Lady," responded Needa. "Those are the words of the gods. That is all I know. There are more in the temple."

Lira looked at her sharply. She felt Needa was not being completely honest with her. So. she asked, "You told me last night not even a bug could get in my rooms, true?"

"Yes, my Lady," Needa answered.

Lira looked at her, then decided, for the first time, to speak about the caress. She could not explain why, but right now seemed like the best time to discuss it.

"May we breakfast? I have a matter I would discuss with you."

"Of course, my Lady. You honor me." Needa replied.

As they walked, Lira thought about what she wanted to say. She was alone here and completely dependent on these people. She did not wish to offend them, or worse, sound like she was insane. Without Ian, she had no claim to anything beyond what they attributed to her.

Needa turned to Lira, "Would you like to dine on the terrace?"

"That would be lovely Needa." Fresh air sounded divine at the moment.

Needa bowed and called to her son Slade. Lira could not understand what they were saying. She felt like an eavesdropper. Slade hurried away. Needa asked her if she would like to walk the long way to the temple while their breakfast was prepared.

"Yes, I would love too." Lira replied, meaning that, as she pondered what to say to Needa. As they walked past a long set of stairs that led further upwards, Lira marveled at the construction of such an immense structure. How was it built, she wondered? As she was lost in reverie, she failed to notice a light green glow up ahead.

"Do you see that light? The green light?"

"Yes, my lady," Needa replied. "It is the god light." Needa looked at her quizzically. "Do you not have a god light?"

Lira did not know how to answer. "Not like this," she finally replied.

Needa nodded as if that was an acceptable answer. They rounded the corner. She could tell the light came from inside the temple above. Lira felt as if someone was watching her, she turned but there was no one there.

Suddenly, they were in very bright sunlight and the temperature jumped perceptibly. A long table of a lovely warm honey colored wood held glistening fruits. She could detect a hint of wine in the gold vase. Thin slivers of roasted bird with the feathers intact laid about the table. There were beautiful flowers...gardenias, honeysuckle, and wild roses. It was all so intoxicatingly lovely. She sat down on a hanging wooden chair that gave the impression of floating as it cradled you. Lira motioned for Needa to join her. Needa sat down in a smaller leaf designed chair.

"May I serve my Lady?" Lira jumped at the new voice.

"I am sorry. I did not realize anyone else was here."

Needa said, "This is Lida. She is from the village and was picked as suitable to serve, but if you like, I can send for different candidates?"

Lira looked at Lida appraisingly. She seemed familiar. She was strikingly beautiful with blue-black hair, tanned skin, and as she looked up, violet eyes, not exactly the color of Lira's, but the closest she had ever seen. Now her carefully chosen questions fled her mind to make room for a new train of questioning.

She looked at Needa and asked, "She was born and raised here?"

"Yes, my Lady. I myself brought her into this world."

"You are her mother?"

"No, I am her duela."

"And that means?" Lira asked. The question hung in the air.

"I am the person who delivered her. A doctor if you will."

"Ah, I see." Lira responded. "So you know the parents?"

"Yes, my Lady, though her mother died in childbirth."

"I am sorry for your loss," Lira said to Lida. "If you would please."

"Yes, my Queen."

Lira looked sSladetled, saying, "I am not your Queen."

Lida shrugged and looked to Needa.

Needa smiled at the girl, "My Lady will do for now."

Lira shook her head in an affirmative, still watching Lida. The girl was quite lovely.

As Lida poured wine into crystal goblets, you could see the scratch marks on the inside where the crystal had been hollowed out for this purpose. She could not imagine how long that would have taken. The goblets were quite heavy.

Lida, in the meantime, had taken a beautiful gold plate inlaid with turquoise at the pointed ends, and began placing little portions of everything on it, while down on her knees, and presenting it to Lira like an offering. She held it up above her head. Lira took it from her, asking her to dine with them. Needa looked happy with that suggestion. As they all served themselves, a lovely wind instrument started to play. She did not know the music but it was restful. As she eased her hunger and thirst, she thought about what she wanted to know the most.

As she swung lightly in the breeze, she felt a serenity stealing over her. She looked out onto the lush land teeming with all manner of life. It was breathtaking. She wished with all her heart her prince were here to share it with her. Ian would love this meat and mulled wine she thought, distracting herself.

"Needa?" Lira asked. "Has there been a God or a Lord here that looks like our Lord Ian?"

Needa looked her straight in the eyes. "Yes, but not exactly like him. A very tall, white man with gold and silver hair and glowing blue eyes. Quetzal is his messenger and friend."

Lira gasped. "Why would you have sacrificed his pet then to us?"

Needa smiled. "Our god, Tahote, said this would be the test to know if he or his descendant had truly returned. He erected this building. Have you not noticed Quetzal is among the carvings and in the paintings? Where you not going to ask me about Quetzal's light?"

"Yes," Lira replied. "I had no idea it was Quetzal's light. He disappeared! Did he go to retrieve my Lord?"

"Who can know the will of a god? Did you ask that of him?"

Lira thought for a moment. "Yes, I did, and he winked out of existence. I have not seen him since, have you?"

"No, my lady."

Lida looked up and said, "Quetzal maybe a trickster, but I believe for such an honest and sincere person, he would offer aid."

Lira was taken aback by Lida's remark. "Well, thank you, Lida. That is very kind of you to say. I hope to hear from my Lord, Prince Ian soon. I am so worried for him."

Lida looked up. "May I ask where he is a prince, my Lady?"

Lira responded, "A far off land called Atlantis. It is a beautiful place surrounded by the most beautiful waters you can imagine. It has three concentric rings of homes...fishing villages on the outside, and the further you go in the circles, the whiter the buildings are with gold tops. There are azure blue waters, and many places you go to by boat. The healers and the oracles are in the innermost ring with the palace of my Prince Ian. His father ruled there; King Minos. A terrible sickness swept over the land to which I was immune, so I went to the palace to help."

As Needa nodded and Lida looked spellbound, she continued. "I met him in the throne room. He was so handsome. I thought him a god himself. Our Golden God of the sky Apollo. He requested I go to his chambers so he would have his own healer. I thought him spoiled for that. I cared for the wellbeing of the people that took me in, and I wanted to help. The gods seemed to do battle from the sea to the earth and into the sky. Great bursts of flame erupted from the earth and rattled the palace. Water swallowed the land. When we went through the room where we met the king, the palace was in shambles. I do not think there is an Atlantis to return to."

Lida looked at her, "My Lady, I wish to ask a question but I do not wish to offend in any way. The gift of your confidence is great, and I am humbled by it."

Lira looked surprised, but said, "You may ask, Lida."

"My Lady, what do you mean by people that took you in? Where you not a princess or an oracle, or wise woman already?"

Lira sighed, same question she always got. "No, I was, if anything, a duela like Needa. I was found as a young child adrift outside the outermost ring of Atlantis. I was alone in a small boat. I have no memory of anything that happened before. All I know was my name was Lira. A nice family took me in. I had brothers and sisters and a mother and father, but they perished from the sickness. They did not have to endure the gods' anger. For that, I am grateful."

"I will pray for the safe return of your Prince, Our King."

"Thank you Lida," Lira said, truly hoping any prayers would bring Ian back to her.

"Needa?"

"Yes, my Lady?"

"When do your gods show themselves?"

"Whenever they decide, my Lady."

"Is there a specific time?" Lira asked.

"Yes," Needa replied, "certain days of the year. We also have temples to our gods not nearly as grand as this, but beautiful nonetheless."

"Did your god, Tahote, give you this test with Quetzal?"

"Yes, my Lady."

"How long ago?"

"Before any remembering of mine. I am one of the elders of this village."

"Truly? You look young, Needa."

"Thank you, my Lady. You have met my son, the leader of our village?"

"Yes, he seems very capable."

"Indeed he is."

"Is there any way to get in touch with your god? How do you pray to him?"

Needa smiled. "There is a prayer room in the temple. I will take you when you're ready."

"Is Lida's family in your village?"

Lida looked at Needa in an almost panicked manner.

"No, I am all she has right now."

"I would like to know more about her after you show me the temple and introduce me to the god that lives there." Lira said.

CHAPTER TWENTY-ONE

Prince Ian
 Ian awoke in the small boat. It looked to be mid-morning. He needed to plot his course to Egypt and was not very sure how far he drifted in the few hours he had slept. He had to find his father and his way back to Lira. He hoped Needa was taking care of her. If anything happened to her, he was not sure what he would do. He had lost his people, his home, his family, his love, and perhaps, were he to admit it, his mind as well. Atlantis surely was not still standing; a ghost city untouched by the gods' war. Maybe he was still dreaming, but how long can a dream last? Perhaps he had caught the sickness and was delirious with fever? That would explain a lot more than what his mind was telling him, but then, he would not have had those amazing hours with Lira!

 He knew in his heart that was real and true. He had to find a way back to her. He grabbed his crystal and lined it up with the sun, unfurling the sail and hoping for the best possible speed. He prayed to Poseidon for help in the mission.

 As he sailed, he thought about the room where he had taken Lira to meet his father. He had told him to bring the thing that mattered the most to him by Midnight, and he had done just that. He loved her from the moment he laid eyes on her. He was quite the ass to her at first to hide the fact that he wanted to take her in his arms and kiss every inch of her and hold her close. The smell of warmed brown sugar and honey was mouthwatering and addicting.

 The place his father sent them to was beautiful beyond words. Except for Atlantis he had never seen a more lush and living landscape. Not in his wildest dreams could he have made that up or the amazing healing grotto where even flowers responded to his every thought. The place seemed familiar but he knew he had never been there. Deja vu, they called it.

As he sailed, he saw aquatic life in the form of sharks, whales, schools of tuna, and a lone sea turtle. What he would not give for some. He had smoked beef and a loaf of unleavened bread. He took a few bites of each and washed it down with a swig of wine from his flagon.

He remembered his father changing right before his eyes. He looked younger and more powerful. His eyes glowed with power. Behind his visage, it had seemed superimposed over an alien countenance. He tried to remember exactly what happened. No matter what he tried, there were gaps in his memory, except for Lira. He remembered every moment with her. It was burned into his memory for all time. What if she needed him? He began to row in his eagerness to get to his father and find a way back to Lira. Perhaps it was the prismatic blue power source in that room in Atlantis. It could not be a one-way trip. How did he get here?

He finally spotted land. Thank you great god Poseidon! His prayers were answered. He drank a bit more wine in celebration. He knew there was a chance he would not find his father, but he had to believe he would. He thought Atlantis gone forever. She stood proud and majestic. Just a ghost town now. Egypt was a desert for a good portion. He would go to Cairo first and inquire about his father. From the Gaza. At least there, gods are familiar. He could pray to Horus for safe passage, Anubis to pass him over, Ra to keep the good weather and wind, Isis to help him find his love, and Seth to send him straight as an arrow to his father.

He would visit every temple on arrival and worship and send sacrifice to each. In a foreign land, it is best to court the Gods' favor. Considering what he had witnessed in the past couple of days, he had no desire whatsoever to see a God angry for any reason. He found a harbor and was pulled in by strong healthy looking young men. He thanked them and gave them some of his bread.

"Can you tell me who is king now?"

They all looked at him as if he had lost his mind.

One spoke broken Greek. "The pharaoh god is Seth Ra."

"Ah, thank you," he replied. "And where might I have words with him?"

One young man nearly choked. Hoping he had not offended them, he looked at the young man who spoke with him.

The young man said, "You cannot talk with the pharaoh, but you can petition the royal house with your case and they will decide what to do from there? What is the problem you have? Maybe we can point you in the right direction."

Ian debated whether to reveal his identity. He had no idea how much these people knew and what they thought and or felt about Atlantis. Well this was as good a place as any, he supposed. The less time wasted the better.

"I am Prince Ian of Atlantis. I came here seeking my father, King Minos. Have you heard of him?"

The young man that spoke to him before now introduced himself. "I am Irea," he said. "We have seen the great man of which you speak. He arrived here on a bolt of lightning. He has not left the palace. He said nothing of a son, but we have seen the gods do many strange things. We do as we are bid." Irea said. "I have never seen a prince travel so humbly."

Ian said, "I should hope not, but how many princes have just lost everything?"

"We have heard the tale of your city," Irea said. "Some even claimed to have seen your gods fighting from where you lived. You must have greatly offended them."

Ian replied, "I know not what happened to make the gods angry, but I intend to have speech with my father. Can you please point me in that direction?"

Irea replied, "I will take you to the palace where they will decide if you see anyone or not."

"Thank you," said Ian. "I appreciate you giving me help."

"It is no trouble," he replied. Irea turned and spoke to his friends and one laughed. The others looked at him with arched eyebrows. Ian began to feel slighted. There was only so much a man could take. He surely did not want to ruin his efforts by offending people, but this was about a true love. He had no time for nonsense from these kids. Irea turned and beheld Ian's eyes. They glowed an electric blue. There seemed to be an outline of a figure superimposed over his own face. Irea and his gang all dropped to their knees.

"I beg you, Prince Ian! We made fun but not in a hostile way my Lord, Prince Ian of Atlantis."

"You have my forgiveness if you can take me to my father."

"Of course my Lord. Please follow me. I will take you to him."

As they tied off his boat, they were quick and their system of pulleys and stays were very efficient. He hoped to reunite with his father quickly, and thereby, with Lira. His stomach began growling rather loudly at this point. One of the men asked if he preferred to go to the tavern first.

As good as a small cup of ale sounded, he replied, "No, thank you. I have great need to hear news of my father."

He grabbed the few things he possessed out of the boat. As he did, it struck him. He had literally gone from prince to pauper in a day. He had no money. No one recognized him or gave him whatever he wished. Good thing he had made friends with the guards and had gone fishing and drinking with them. At least he knew how to interact in some way.

Feeling the burn on his skin, he was sore from rowing. Irea looked at him thoughtfully and from his belt handed him a clay jar stoppered with a rubbery feeling stub. Ian looked at it.

"What is it?"

Irea replied, "It is medicine and will stop the burn that walks across your body. You apply a small amount where it burns, and it will cool and soothe the sting."

Ian opened the jar sniffed it. It did not smell noxious. He scooped out a bit. It had the consistency of a gel. He rubbed it on experimentally. Aww. Relief. Ian thanked Irea for his consideration as he finished coating the burn and handed the bottle back.

Irea said, "You are most welcome. It comes from the aloe plant. It has many uses."

Ian felt relief from the sunburn. "Thank you. I appreciate the use of your medicine. Can we be about the business of finding my father? It is most urgent. If I have any means, I will see you rewarded for all the services you have rendered me."

Irea looked at him, "I have no need for payment, but if you are indeed a prince, perhaps you have need of a servant?"

Ian looked him over. "I would consider it most seriously. As you have heard, I am not in the position to have a servant now. Though I am a prince, I am a prince without a people or a family at this moment. To be brutally honest, I am quite unsure that my memories are accurate. I would trust no one but my father with this tale for now, until I understand what has happened. If you can accept that and perhaps wait for consult with my father, I would surely consider your offer in great earnestness. Do you agree?"

"I think, my Lord, it took great courage and an honest and humbled heart to say all that has transpired and what you freely admit you are unsure of. I admit your boat does not yell royalty to me, but your bearing and speech are cultured. I have no reason to doubt you. I would gladly accept your terms and look forward to the full tale in time. Let us hasten towards the palace and see if we can reunite you with your father or some of your people."

They walked down the crowded dusty street. The adobe and stone houses were tightly packed together. All manner of people and animals ran amuck in the streets with no mind to anyone else around them. Ian marveled at the differences between this city and his home in Atlantis. The people seemed happy here.

The man at the market stall called out, "Love charms! I have love charms the Goddess Isis herself has blessed. No one can refuse you with such potent magic!"

Ian stopped and glanced at the man's wares. "Can you summon a loved one with this charm from anywhere in the world!" The merchant assured him that he could.

Ian said, "How does it work?"

The merchant looked at him. "I do not question the gods, my good man. I am just pleased to be blessed with the results and their favor."

Irea looked at the man than back at Ian. "My Lord has lost someone dear to his heart. When he has rested, perhaps we will come back to visit your wares. What is the cost of such a blessed charm?"

The man looked at them both appraisingly. "For my young Lord here, one gold piece."

Irea nodded, "We shall see. Come my Lord. Were you not in a hurry?"

Ian looked at him blankly. "Yes, I was."

He was thinking of those amazing violet eyes. They seemed to be haunting him. He needed to get back to his father. Lira had to be real! He had to find her. Surely, he had not finally found love, just to lose it again so quickly.

People filled the streets and called out their wares from market stalls. The smell of roast duck made his mouth water, but he had no time for that. What if Lira was in danger, or his father, or even worse yet, Lira was not real? His stomach clenched painfully at that thought. All thoughts of hunger evaporated.

"Irea, is there a faster way to go, by chance?"

"There is," Irea replied, "but, it is perilous, full of thieves, murderers, rapists, and worse." Ian pondered for a moment. What could be worse than thieves, rapists, and murderers? Warlocks and slave traders maybe.

Irea looked at him patiently as the throng of people moved around them. "I do not think it is a good idea to go that way, being only two of us. Perhaps, you have magic on your side you have not mentioned yet. I would like to fulfill my promise to you with the least peril for us both."

Ian could not argue with that logic. Defeated and deflated, he said to Irea, "You are right of course, this is your city. I do not know it. Please lead the quickest, safest route you know, because I am still not sure I am in my right mind."

Irea acknowledged that with a bow of his head but said nothing. They began moving again. As Ian watched the people around him, he noticed they were predominantly of one race it seemed, but there were other people here. Nubians he had only heard about. Fierce they looked, just standing and talking to each other with their hand always resting on a knife, sword, or a whip. The Egyptians themselves seemed happy and were olive skinned with dark penetrating eyes. Some seemed fierce, most just normal people.

He asked Irea, "Is this normal for your kingdom?"

Irea shook his head in the negative. "This is the more nobles of our kingdom. This is a prosperous place indeed. Many hope to apprentice at one of the shops. To do so is to have a full belly every night, and to send some money home if needs be. That is how I came here."

Ian looked at him a renewed interest. "What did you apprentice in?"

Irea replied, "Writing. I hoped to one day to work in the temples, writing the will of the Gods, or dispatching messages from the priests. It was an unrealistic dream."

He trailed off and did not seem inclined to go on.

Ian decided now was not the time to prod the man helping him to find his father. If he truly wished to serve him before that oath was taken, Ian would find out all he needed to know. As they walked, a majestic statue appeared, carved from a red granite stone. It was as big as any structure he had yet seen.

"Irea," he inquired, "is that one of your Gods?"

"Yes and no. He is a God King, his name is Horus."

"Ah. I have not heard much of your lands, forgive my ignorance."

Irea inclined his head. "I do not consider you ignorant in any way, my Lord. I think you have been through a calamity unprecedented in my knowing. Perhaps you just need rest and food. I think a lot will return to you in time."

Ian replied, "I thank you. I hope you prove correct. I thought my father would be in a land much further away, but somehow, I knew to come here. I hope he has the answers I need."

Ian thought silently. *Lira has to be real, and I must find a way back to her. Dear gods, do not let her be hurt or in danger in any way.* Ian was still lost in thoughts of his home and the woman he loved, following Irea blindly.

Irea stopped and said to someone, "My Lord is here to see the visitor that arrived yesterday."

Ian looked around Irea and saw a guard who stood in front of a counsellor, possibly a priest. The person in question seemed to know Irea and whom his father was, if that was the person who arrived yesterday. This was all in the open but it also seemed very secretive.

"Please come in and refresh my Lord, and when he is seen too, you may go to the kitchen and see what they have for you."

Irea said, "I thank you. Where should my Lord wait?"

"In the second inner chamber," the man replied. "I will post a guard as well."

Irea bowed, and the man with the dark braided hair, gold torque necklace, and white linen robe hurried off before Ian caught his name.

Irea turned to him. "My Lord Ian, if you would follow me, I will get you settled with some food and clean clothes before you meet with your father."

Ian replied, "I would be grateful."

As they walked through the palace, a guard followed behind them. It was very quiet for a palace, Ian thought. Lights flickered here and there, casting shadows on the colored walls. The further in they moved, the more Ian noticed he had seen some of these colored figures before.

Then Irea stopped and gestured him into a room. It was enormous. The ceilings were surely three houses tall with the heavens caught upon them as if by magic. He marveled at the beauty. The middle of the room was a long table filled with all manner of bowls and vases. Some had food. Some had wine. Others had scented oils. His stomach growled impatiently. Irea quirked an eyebrow.

"Would you like to bathe first or eat my Lord?"

"Bathe please."

A woman came from behind a curtain and bowed to him. She was dressed the same as the last person he had seen. They must be priests, he thought. She gestured towards the curtain. Ian inclined his head and followed her. There was a small bathing space carved into the floor. Water spilled from above, like a rainstorm pattering into the basin. The woman left clean linens and a drying cloth. There was also soap and oil of lilac and sandalwood.

Ian stripped off his filthy garments and stepped under the rain shower. It felt heavenly as he soaped up and realized how much he stank. How could anyone think him a Lord, much less a prince? Amused for a moment, he hurried his rain shower. He hoped to see his father soon. The sooner the better. He dried himself and thought this place was indeed strange. No servants to help him. Well that was fine. He did not know their customs here. He dressed and hurried out, leaving the clothes behind.

Irea smiled, sitting in the middle of the table. "That is a vast improvement over your first appearance."

"Thank you Irea," he said with a smile. "It is a vast improvement. Let us break bread together while we wait."

Irea said, "Do you know the foods on the board?"

"Not all," admitted Ian. "I will trust your judgment."

"Ah, I am honored then."

Irea grabbed a gold plate and put fish, olives, crusted bread, grapes, and bananas on it along with a sweet wine in a gold goblet. Ian fell to the meal with great zeal. His stomach grumbling thankfully.

"Irea?" Ian inquired. "Do you know where my father is?"

"Actually my Lord, I do not know for sure the visitor is your father. Although he looks much like you, he was injured when he was brought here. He had blue lightning crackling around him, everyone was afraid to go near him. He asked if this was the Amazon. What a strange question I thought. 'No, this is the Nile,' I replied to him. 'Are you lost, my Lord,' I asked him. He replied, 'Yes, lost. Everything is lost now, and collapsed.' The priests were called and the guards brought him here."

Ian stood, "You did not tell me he was injured!"

"I did not tell you he was your father, either." Irea said.

"I want to see him now," Ian said in a deadly serious tone.

Irea looked at him askance. "Did I not arrange for that very thing the moment we arrived? I said I was looking for a good man to serve. Not a spoiled brat."

Ian lunged across the table at Irea. "How dare you insult me!" Ian raged, his face mottled red from anger.

Irea said, "You have no proof of who you are, yet I took you at your word. You will not take me at mine? I just told you all I know of the stranger that arrived here. Perhaps it would be wise to wait to kill me, till you find out who he is."

"I know who he is!" Ian yelled. "I know no one else who commands blue lightning."

"Really?" said Irea. "Your father commands energies like the gods?" Ian deflated somewhat, not sure how to proceed.

"I regret my outburst. I have lost my entire civilization. My father being here would be a gift from the gods. Please forgive me. I overstepped your gracious hospitality."

Ian sat back down, grabbed some sugared dates and began to eat them as he contemplated what Irea had told him, and what he remembered. Tiny bits of things had been coming to him all day...the room in Atlantis, the fantastic tale of space travel, Lira's face as his father described who and what they were and what was happening.

Lira. Ian's heart clenched again at the thought of her alone. He could still smell and taste her warm brown sugar and honey flavor, the way her violet eyes darkened with desire, the flare of her hips, and the saucy attitude hidden underneath it all. *My gods, it must have all happened.* His heart said it is so. *What could have gone so wrong?*

The last thing he remembered, he had fallen asleep in a lovely open-air hut after making love to Lira. How she must feel waking without him? Did she feel as lost as he? She never voiced her feelings for him.

As Ian mused quietly, Irea watched him surreptitiously. *I think he is the one I have been told to wait for, but something is not right with him. I glimpse the person inside like a superimposed picture over his features. We shall see when our visitor gets here.*

CHAPTER TWENTY-TWO

King Minos

"My Lord Minos?" The priest bowed to the man sitting before him at a table, busily writing with great concentration.

"Yes?" King Minos replied.

"You have a visitor."

King Minos looked astounded. "Who would know I am here? Have some of my people survived?"

"That I do not know, my Lord. This visitor claims a closer relationship to you."

"Who?"

"My Lord, he claims to be your son."

"What? Take me to him immediately."

"Of course, this way."

He bowed and led the way down the arch lined hallways.

Gods, thought Minos. *What could have gone wrong? He should be in South America with Lira, and what about her? They said, only my son. Surely, nothing has happened this quickly. Well, of course something happened if he is here in a day. Only the portals could make travel like that possible.*

They thought him a god here. He did not want to disabuse them of that notion. He needed somewhere to stay to write his people's' history. What better place than a fount of learning and information like Egypt. There was so much to do. He still had to travel. He had depended on Ian to take over some of the teachings that needed passing on. The source of power for Atlantis lay within their blood and their minds. So many had given their lives to pass on the knowledge. Atlantis was gone now, but she would never be forgotten, if he had anything to say about it.

If only Ian had children, his line and the knowledge would have been more secure. That's why he had pushed so hard for a marriage. The universe had a grand plan for all. Perhaps Lira was what the great powers had waited on. There was something different about her. She seemed god-touched if he was any judge. Could Ian have offended her gods? What could have happened?

He remembered the trip to Earth. The long sleep and all his people that were lost along the way. Ian's mother, Kia, had survived with him but had died in childbirth. No knowledge he possessed nor gods on earth could save her. She was his beautiful and gracious wife. He could never replace her, so he never tried. He threw himself into this new world. He designed and helped build Atlantis. Part of the bottom of the city was part of the ship they came in. All of the knowledge stored there, lost to a volcano and a tsunami that left nothing. In one day and night, it was gone. Strangely enough, the gods of this world saw the destruction of Atlantis. Their oracle prophesied three days until it was gone, and it was true. He could not go back and check for some time. Well enough. It was time to find out what happened and if his son was truly here.

He hurried on behind the priest. They stopped in front of a guard. The priest spoke to him, and he stepped aside. King Minos walked into the room and saw a familiar blonde head. He began to choke with emotion, "Ian?"

Ian turned around, quickly dropping a date. "Father!" Ian cried.

"Yes, my son. What are you doing here? I sent you somewhere else! What has happened? Where is Lira?"

Ian sagged in relief. "She is real. She is..."

Minos looked at his son. "What are you saying?"

"Lira, she is real!" he said it with such joy in his voice.

"Why would you think otherwise, Ian?" Minos asked impatiently. "I was with you in a room in Atlantis then there was a blue light and a doorway."

King Minos patted his son on the back. "Enough for now. We need to find privacy for your memories. We will discuss them. Have no worries on that. Are you unharmed my son?"

Ian replied, "I have a big lump on my head and some bruises I sustained in the fall of our city."

"Hmm," King Minos intoned. "And who is this you sup with Ian?"

"Irea, may I introduce you to my father, King Minos of Atlantis. Father, this is my soon to be servant and already friend, Irea. He rescued me from the boat I came in."

King Minos raised an eyebrow at that. "I am indebted to you for saving my son and bringing him to me. Was he alone?"

Irea replied, "Yes, King Minos, quite alone. He did not even have a servant to row the boat. I was there when you came out of the water as well, good king, quite a sight, both of you. Your son was not so charged as you, my King."

King Minos looked the young man over appraisingly. "You will be a good friend to my son and keep him from any dangers with your life. All our secrets become yours upon pain of death of the most horrible kind. Staked out in the desert with no water, no food, left there to turn into a mummy or food for whatever wanders by. Do you swear on this?"

Irea walked around the table and knelt and the men's feet. "Yes, I do swear my allegiance to your house as protector and friend."

"Very well, rise." King Minos replied. "I would now give you a gift that comes with a mark. Do you accept?"

"Yes, my King," Irea replied.

King Minos pulled out a glowing blue rock from his pouch that hung at his hip. "You will gain knowledge to help mankind and this family. It will be unfamiliar to you; do you still accept?"

"Yes," Irea replied without hesitation.

Ian looked back and forth. Never had he heard of this from his father before? Why would it hurt? What knowledge?

His father reached out his hand with the stone in it. He brushed back the hair at Irea's temple with his other hand. "Are you ready?"

Irea nodded. He pressed the glowing blue stone to Irea's temple. Irea cried out in pain. Prismatic blue light shot through the room. Ian closed his eyes against a wave of memories he could not quite hold on to. Still the light pulsed. Irea was barely murmuring now.

King Minos asked, "Irea, can you hear me?"

"Yes, my King."

"Do you see now?"

"With wondrous clarity and humility, my Lord King."

"What is needed is a protector and keeper. Can you do this?" King Minos asked.

"I think I was born for this," Irea replied.

"Thank you Irea," King Minos said, removing his hands. Irea still knelt on the floor.

Ian asked, "Father, what did you do to him?"

"Ian, I do not know what has happened, but you need a protector. As you clearly do not remember our real people, I have given Irea the information you will need to access at some point when you are healed."

"Why could you not use the stone to just give it to me then?" Ian asked. "I have a thousand questions. I have no idea what is real and what is a fever dream or a blow to the head."

King Minos said, "Ian, the knowledge is there. You may not have access to it for many reasons. Let us begin puzzling this out."

"What about Irea? He has not moved. Is he alright?" Ian asked.

"Yes, he is fine." King Minos replied. "It is much for a human mind to process. He had to shut down nonessentials to absorb it all. There is something different in this young man as well as your lovely Lira."

"Yes! I was with Lira in a beautiful land with a pyramid that reached to the skies! The next thing I remember, I was back in Atlantis, but no one was there. It was empty of all living things, but everything was still there physically. I even saw a boat in the distance. I found the boat and traveled, unlocking each gate of each ring to get here."

King Minos looked at him, "Let us sit. I would like some wine whilst I hear your story."

"Of course Father, let me get it for you. This is a strange place we are in, is it not? I have not seen servants. Priests perhaps?"

"Yes, we are in the priests' temple. They thought I was a god, so they brought me here. I have not disabused them of this idea either. It is a safe and quiet place."

"But father, you were to be in the Amazon."

"Yes, well you were to be in South America. Let us sSladet with your story."

"Well, I told you what I remember," Ian said.

"Did you spend any amount of time in the land with Lira?"

"Yes, a night and part of a day. The natives said we came to the temple on a blue bolt of lightning and that we hand been foretold."

"Interesting," King Minos mused. "Who told you this?"

"A native woman named Needa. She seems to be a wise woman, and her son was chief of the village, his name was Slade."

"Besides you showing up, what did they foretell?" King Minos asked.

"That a light haired man would come from the heavens and bring the new age of learning and peace for many hundreds of years to come. Also, that water is sacred to this god/man. He can bring the rain and make the crops grow. Make the land hospitable again. That his woman would be fertility incarnate and mother to them all."

"You remember quite a bit?"

"It just rushed out of me." Ian replied.

"So, after this woman and her son met you, were you with Lira?"

"Yes, the whole time till I woke in Atlantis."

"Is it possible you upset someone there? You woke in a giant white pyramid they called their gods' temple?"

"Yes, father."

"Did you sense the presence of any other beings? Mayhap a god you did not honor? And he sent you back to where you came from?"

"Father, who could do that?"

"Ian, I have been here hundreds of years. There are more beings with powers than you know. We have learnings and powers but we still prayed to gods did we not?"

"Yes, we did Father, but it seems hypocritical now."

"No, my son, you will always worship a god or be setup as one yourself. In a foreign land, is it not better to learn your surroundings as they learn from you?"

Ian took a sip of wine thinking about that. He looked over at Irea. "How long will he be like this?"

"I cannot tell you." King Minos said simply. "I have never trusted a human with that much knowledge."

"Are we not human?" Ian asked.

"We have had this conversation before, Ian. Give your mind a rest. It will come to you. Yes, in a way we are. Short answer my son; I would prefer you back where I sent you because it is vital that we establish networks around the world."

"Then why are you here instead of the Amazon?" Ian asked.

"Because I did not expect you to choose a person as the thing you could not live without by Midnight. I did not have enough energy to get myself that far."

"But father, Atlantis still stands! The room is intact everything unblemished."

King Minos shook his head, "I think perhaps you were sent to a mirror image, maybe another dimension where Atlantis exists where no one can find it."

There was a rustling sounded behind them, then a polite cough.

"I am sorry to interrupt. May I have some wine? I have a mighty headache."

King Minos laughed, and handed Irea the vase.

"Do you remember anything?" Ian asked anxiously.

"Indeed," Irea said. "Some completely unbelievable, but I know them to be true. If I can help you get back to where you need to be my prince, I will use all at my disposal. I will travel to this land and help you build there. It looks like visions I have had since childhood. I knew when I met you, the gods willed it."

King Minos said gravely, "If you do this, you will leave everyone and everything you know behind for a world you know nothing of."

"Yes, my king, I do understand. I have no obligations here."

"Very well," the king replied. "We are trying to ascertain what happened to Ian. How he got to an empty Atlantis, and by boat, to here. I am of the opinion it is an angry god of South America. What do you think Irea?"

"Well, my Lord, it seems that would be the only way. He cannot have traveled from South America to Atlantis without a portal in this short of a time, and not to mention, Atlantis is gone."

"Good points, Irea," King Minos replied. "Now how do we get Ian back to his lady love and not upset the gods that live there?"

"I would suggest the supplicant's approach."

"Which god do we pray too then?"

"My Lord, I would ask this Needa. She seems to be around a lot. Is there anything you can remember that might have offended the gods, Prince Ian?"

"We had sex in the pyramid temple. It was mind blowingly good. It seemed that everything in the room was there to help us...even the heated pool of water felt like massaging fingers, and Lira seemed more in her element. More of everything. A beautiful bird helped us find our way out and then disappeared. When Needa showed up, her son had a similar bird that he wanted to sacrifice it to us. Lira would have none of it. She made it her pet and called it Quetzal. You don't think the bird is a god? We saved it!"

"Right now Ian, none of us know. We need to get you back there," King Minos replied.

"Yes father, I need to find Lira at once. I hope the natives are treating her well. I cannot lose her."

"You will not, my son. If Irea has seen her, then you are destined."

Irea inclined his head. "I have seen her. I would prepare for a journey now if you permit, my Lords?"

"Yes, Irea I would appreciate that," Ian replied.

Irea left to see about provisions.

"Father, can we not use a portal? This journey will take weeks. Who knows what will happen to her in the meantime?"

"My son, if I find a way to use a portal, I will send you through it, but as far as I know, this rock is all that is left of the power of Atlantis."

CHAPTER TWENTY-THREE

Lira

Lira was extremely worried about Ian. *Why has he not returned? Maybe he is injured. Please gods, let him be well! Quetzal just popped out of existence. I did ask him to find Ian. What could take so long?*

A light brush against her cheek felt reassuring. At least the caress was with her. Needa and Lida talked across the room. They were spinning something maybe wool.

Lida smiled at her reassuringly. "I can see the gods smile on you my Lady."

"Really? What do you see?"

"I see a golden god standing behind you. He just touched your cheek."

Lira was amazed. *How could she have known? Ian did not even seem to notice the caress during their amour .*

"You are a blessed daughter of Tekal!"

"I do not know who I am a daughter of. I was found floating in a boat outside Atlantis."

Needa said, "Lida is never wrong. She is a seer for our people and is gifted by the gods. That is why she was chosen to serve you my Lady."

"Lida," Lira asked, "Do you wish to serve? Or would you rather be with your people or a husband?"

"No, my lady. I would love to serve. As you know, I have no family. No husband, though there is a man I dream about."

"Well don't we all!" Needa laughed. "Tell us about your dream man?"

"Yes, Lida," Lira chimed in.

"Alright, you gang up on me though! He comes from a land far away. He has dark hair, and the deepest dark brown eyes I could sSladee into forever. He is tan and has a scar."

"Well that's dreamy." Needa laughed, "What about the good parts?"

Lida looked at her and said evenly, "I have never gotten that far."

Needa started laughing so hard, she was snorting. Lira began to laugh and so did Lida. After the giggling bout subsided, Needa said, "Still a virgin even in your dreams. A shame those looks are going to waste. You should marry Slade."

Lida said, "I do not mean any ill will, but I will not. My destiny lies with Lira."

Needa smiled, picking up the yarn. "Mine too, Lida."

Lira silently thanked any gods listening for these two wonderful women. She kept looking at the jungle below praying to see a blonde head pop out any moment. So far no luck.

"Lida, if you can foretell, can you see Lord Ian coming back to me?" Lira asked.

"Yes, my Lady he comes back."

"When? When Lida? Is he ok?"

"My Lady, I do not know the exact details, but I see him in your future as brightly as I see Tekal standing behind you!"

"What?" Lira whirled around searching for the mysterious Tekal.

"Have you ever heard of Tekal going from this land to another far away?"

Lida replied, "Of course. He must visit all his children."

"Umm, I'm pretty sure he doesn't think of me as his child."

Lida said, "It does not actually mean child, necessarily. Perhaps you were chosen to bear his child?"

"Yes, well, I would like a say in that. I only plan to have children with my Lord Ian."

Needa smiled, "As the gods will it."

Lira was feeling extremely restless now. "I am going to the grotto for a soak."

"Do you wish us to accompany you?" Lida asked.

"No, I would like to be alone for a bit."

Needa and Lida inclined their heads.

Lira began the descent into the temple. She could smell the water and the fragrance of the lovely flowers. She blushed to think about how they were last used. She missed Ian so badly. Where could he be?

She got undressed and stepped into the pool. She sank in, her bottom hitting the ledge, her head leaning back, and her hair fanned out in a beautiful disarray around her. She felt the caress brush against her temples.

"I mean no disrespect to you, Lord Tekal, but I do not wish to be your vessel for your child. I await my Lord Ian."

"Lira," a disembodied voice said right by her ear.

She jumped. "Lira?"

It was Ian! "Oh! Ian, I hear you. Where are you?"

"My love, I'm trying to reach you, but there is something or someone blocking my path. Can you find out what gods to pray to or sacrifice to?"

"You! You did this! You sent him away from me, did you not, Lord Tekal! Answer me! Did you send him away?"

"Yes," a whisper came. "You were meant for me."

"No, or I would have been here. Can you take form and talk to me?"

"No, not enough of my children believe in me."

"Well, you're not helping your cause here."

Lira sat and thought. Feeling like a prune, she got out of the water and walked over to the grotto where she and Ian made glorious love two nights ago. Then she had an idea.

"Lord Tekal? Are you still here?"

"Yes."

"Can we strike a deal?" Nothing. She plunged ahead. "I could guarantee you more followers and true believers. Once a year we would sacrifice whatever you require, be it blood, statues, or a woman for your seed, as long as she volunteers. As the rulers here, we could make them remember you. What say you?"

"What do you need?" a soft voice said by her ear.

"That you let Lord Ian back into this land and no more extracurricular activity with me."

"You would swear on your unborn children's lives?"

Lira heard a female voice clearly. She tied her robe shut and turned. There was Lida walking trance like towards her.

"Do you swear this to be true? I will take your children and smash them on my temple if you lie."

Lira was shaking, but she was determined. "Yes, I swear and Ian will as well."

"And the other?" Lida intoned.

Lira looked confused. "What other?" she asked.

"The man tied to your Lord's soul. Protector they whisper."

"I don't know him, but he will swear or I will cut his throat myself."

Lida said, "A deal is struck, blood is needed to bring your Lord home."

"My blood? Gladly!"

"Yes, and more." Lida said.

Chills ran through her body. "How much more?" Lira asked.

"Three people will suffice." Lida responded.

"Do you need all their blood?"

"No, a cut that bleeds quickly and heals easily."

"Alright, I will return shortly. You will wait for me here?"

"Yessss," the voice answered, sibilantly.

At once, Lida seemed to have awoken. "My Lady? Why am I here?"

"Lord Tekal took you over to make a deal. I heard Ian! He is trying to get back to me! Let us run upstairs. We need Needa."

She had never thought she could run steps faster than she did the other day, but today she nearly flew.

"Needa," she called, breathing heavily from exertion.

Lida finally caught up to her as well.

"I want to ask a favor. You must do it willingly, so if you do not, please do not say you will."

"My Lady?" Needa asked, "What do you need?"

"I need a blood sacrifice from three people. While I was in the pool, I heard Ian call out to me. He said a God was keeping him from coming back. Then, Lida showed up talking in a strange tone. Lord Tekal was using her to communicate. He wishes to have true believers again, and sacrifices, and maybe have a child. I do not know. I just want Lord Ian back."

Lida spoke up then. "I already believe in Lord Tekal. I will help you."

Needa said, "I too, believe. I will also help you."

"Thank you." she kissed them each on the cheek.

"Please, can we hurry? Lira pleaded.

Three woman descended the temple stairs to make a blood deal with a god. Bravery, like Lira had never seen. They did not even ask how much blood. She was incredibly grateful. They stopped at the pool.

"Lord Tekal?" Lira asked.

"I am here," drawn out words sounded softly. "There is a silver knife and bowl. You will each decide where to cut. Blood must flow quickly for this to work."

Lira grabbed the knife. Lida and Needa stood with her. She sliced her left inner forearm and held it over the bowl. She handed the knife to Needa, who cut the palm of her right hand and held it over the bowl. Lida then cut by her hairline, holding her head somewhat over the bowl. Her cut was bleeding profusely. The other women looked at her askance. "Head wounds bleed greatly." No one knew what to say to that.

"Lord Tekal, we have done our part. Will you honor us with yours?"

"Yes..." he whispered.

All the blood in the bowl began to smoke and bubble. It rose as a red mist, then gaining light to a light pink.

Pop! Quetzal appeared!

"Where have you been my friend?" Lira asked.

Just then. "Lira is that you? Is it safe to come through?"

"Ian, is it a pink to reddish doorway?"

"Yes! With light shining."

"Hurry before anything else happens."

Next thing she knew, there was Ian, dressed in strange robes, but her Ian!

"Please do not leave me again." Lira pleaded, tears rolling down her cheeks.

"Lira, my love, I would never willingly leave you. Don't you realize how much I love you?"

"Ian! Oh Ian! I love you, too!" she sobbed.

He picked her up and cuddled her to his chest. "It's ok, little blossom, I am here."

As everyone watched the emotional scene before them, no one seemed to notice when a second man stepped out from the portal. Lida looked at him and fainted. Needa turned to see what was wrong. Maybe she had lost too much blood.

Lira ran to her friend, "Lida? Please!"

Lira began telling Ian about the deal she had made. "Please, do not hate me Ian? It is not so bad. Everyone has gods, right?"

Ian was nodding, looking concerned at Lida, when Needa let out a yelp.

Lira and Ian turned to see Irea standing there.

"I am sorry, Irea, I had no idea you came with me."

"I can see why," looking at Lira. Then he said, "May I render some aid to your friend, my Lady?"

Lira looked at Ian, "...and he is?"

"He is my friend and protector and yours as well. Irea, meet my soon to be wife, Lira. Lira, this is Irea."

"So this is the other I bargained for." Lira said.

Irea looked at her in puzzlement.

"We all used our blood with a god called Lord Tekal to let you back in this realm. It was he who whisked you away from me."

As Lira began explaining, Lida woke up and sSladeed into the darkest brown eyes, and smiled, "It is you."

Irea looked back at her. "Well I guess I am glad then. Thank you for the gift to bring my Lord Ian back home. Let me help you up."

As their fingers touched, a green lightning spark went through the room. Everyone was sSladetled.

Ian said, "I guess more introductions are in order."

Lira said, "Ian, meet my friend and oracle, Lida."

"It is very nice to meet you, Lida," Ian replied.

"Needa, this is Irea my friend and protector. Now that everyone knows everyone, perhaps we could go upstairs so I might show Irea our new home."

"More stairs," Lira grumbled.

Ian swung her up in his arms. "I will carry you, little blossom."

"Oh Ian, how I have missed you!"

"I was only gone a day!"

"Well, to me, it felt like ten years."

"Maybe I can make it up to you later?" Ian smirked.

"Is that an invitation or a threat?"

"Both, little blossom, both. You do like flowers, do you not," he said with a sly grin.

"Ian you know I do! I think we should test that out again."

Lira was gorgeous when she blushed, Ian thought. Finally, at the top of the temple, he gently laid Lira on the cushioned throne and waited for Irea. Some time went by. Finally, a disheveled Irea turned up.

"Where have you been?" Ian asked.

"I noticed some of the characters and coloring that looked almost the same as in Cairo. I was examining them. Extraordinary."

Ian radiated satisfaction at his friend's response. "I had the same reaction. What do you think Irea? Could this be our new home? A new birthplace for Atlantis?"

"Do not forget the deal with Lord Tekal!" Lira said. "I would hate to have to gut you myself, but a promise is a promise, especially to a god."

"Oh yes, my Lady. This is a great land. Worshipping the god who lives here will be no hardship." He looked over at Lida who smiled and looked down. "No hardship at all."

Back in Cairo, King Minos watched his son and his protector go through a portal he did not make. Clearly, more of his race survived then he thought.

He must be careful. The tale of Atlantis needed to be a warning to those who would try to abuse power and anger the gods. That would be the story he would write.

The most important information about Atlantis is that it is between worlds and biding its time.

END

Thank you for reading this book. If you enjoyed it, please consider leaving a review at your favorite retailer.

Thanks.

Printed in Great Britain
by Amazon